PRAISE FOR *WAITING FOR THE BULLET*

'Madeleine D'Arcy's stories are funny and wry and pulsate with all the mad rude energies of life itself but often there is an undercurrent of darkness or sadness just beneath the surface and this is what deepens and gives real weight to the work. A very accomplished collection.'
   — Kevin Barry, author of *Dark Lies the Island* (Jonathan Cape)

'Madeleine D'Arcy's stories simply sizzle with wit and hilarity. But between the many laugh-out-loud moments, there's a poignant undertow that will break your heart.'
   — Mary Morrissy, author of *The Rising of Bella Casey* (O'Brien Press)

'I greatly enjoyed Madeleine D'Arcy's supple and finely worked short stories, for their skillfulness, their sense of organisation and their quiet intelligence. Most of all, I liked the delicate transmission that these are stories: records of the exceptional, with something to say.'
   — Joseph O'Connor, author of *Where Have You Been?* (Harvill Secker)

'These stories are wry and funny. They speak of life as it is now. The truths Madeleine D'Arcy tells aren't pretty but her sympathy and insight are gigantic.'
   — Carlo Gèbler, author of *The Dead Eight* (New Island)

'The stories in *Waiting for the Bullet* brim with energy. Madeleine D'Arcy has brought together a collection of people who are real, living — or sometimes simply existing — breathing, fighting the good fight, and they, in turn, have brought their tales of love and loss and laughter, their achievements and their disappointments. Most importantly, in the midst of all this energy, she has the courage and the talent of the great writer — the courage to allow her characters to pause, to fail, to recognise their frailties and the talent to follow them, unnervingly, as they muddle through the shadows that inevitably fall.

This is a mesmerising collection, beautifully written and ringing with the truth.'
— **John MacKenna, author of** *The Space Between Us* **(New Island)**

'Madeleine D'Arcy's stories are wonderfully witty, with a feather-light touch to offset their disquieting darkness. An original and exciting new voice.'
— **Martina Evans, author of** *No Drinking, No Dancing, No Doctors* **(Bloomsbury)**

'Madeleine D'Arcy's stories have that rare quality of being instantly readable while leaving an enduring resonance. She mines a recognisable contemporary world of high streets, dinner parties, train journeys and Pot Noodles, yet invests these familiar scenarios with her own quirkiness and originality. Her prose is nothing less than smooth and inviting, her ear for dialogue spot on. These are tales that grip the imagination and deepen our empathy with the human condition.'
— **James Harpur, author of** *Angels and Harvesters* **(Anvil)**

'Madeleine D'Arcy is a rueful and ironic observer of human uncertainty and misunderstandings, and of the nuances of speech by which characters give themselves away—a natural short story writer capable of creating the sense of a world in a few thousand words.'
— **Ciaran Carty, author of** *Intimacy with Strangers* **(Lilliput)**

'A collection of memorable, well-wrought, sometimes hard-edged, love stories—of love gone wrong, of what we can mistake for love—deftly delivered by D'Arcy's wise, witty and impressively assured narrative voice.'
— **Anthony Glavin, author of** *Nighthawk Alley* **(New Island)**

WAITING FOR THE BULLET

WAITING FOR THE BULLET
Short Fiction

Madeleine D'Arcy

Doire Press

First published in March, 2014.

Doire Press
Aille, Inverin
Co. Galway
www.doirepress.com

Layout: Lisa Frank
Proofreading: Fiona Nic Dhonnacha
Cover design: John MacMonagle, Raven Design
Author photo: Andrew Lane

Printed by Clódóirí CL
Casla, Co. na Gaillimhe

ISBN 978-1-907682-34-6

Published with the assistance of The Arts Council / An Chomhairle Ealaíon.

CONTENTS

For Andrew and Cass

CLOCKING OUT

It was only my second day on the job and the bus had been slow. I was in a right tizzy as I rushed along the corridor, afraid I'd be late. Just as I reached the clocking-in machine, there he was, right beside me — the life and soul of the factory floor, or so he already seemed, to me.

'The new girl, is it?' he said.

I said yes, shyly. I was distracted. I looked up and down the rack of brown clock-in cards and it seemed to take forever to find mine. Finally I grabbed it and shoved it into the machine. Only a minute left. Nothing happened. I was going to be in trouble. Someone would probably give out to me.

'Feck,' I muttered.

He took it out of my hands. 'You have it the wrong way round, you eejit,' he laughed, and leaned against me as he shoved it in. He knew how to do it right.

The machine made a clicking noise and he pretended to give the card back to me twice, which confused me.

'Smile,' he said. 'It's not the end of the world.'

I had to leave that job. That's why I'm here in London. I'm on my way to work now, on the Piccadilly Line. There's a trendy couple sitting opposite me. They have money and they're smart. You know it by the look of them. He has a nice shirt and jeans, and the kind of shoes called 'casual' even though they cost just as much as Sunday shoes. She's wearing clothes that seem almost colourless and plain, but they're not *plain* plain, if you know what I mean. They're classy. You wouldn't find that kind of gear back home where I'm from. This man and woman — I'm not jealous of them. At least I don't think so. I just wish I had a bit more cop-on, that's all. I wish I had known the things I needed to know in life at the time I should have known them. I mean, it's obvious those two people are well clued-in, not thick like me. They'd laugh to think that anyone could be as foolish as I was. They'd be sick laughing to think that a curly-haired chancer who wore grey polyester trousers and patterned jumpers and worked as the floor manager in a factory could make someone demented with love. But I didn't know any better then. No one ever gave me the time of day before. I was crazy about him.

He sang, as he went around the desks, checking that we were all working. Sometimes he sang a song off the radio, about being in love with two different women and feeling like a fool. He winked at me while he sang. He had a lovely singing voice. But I was the fool, not him.

I used to sit behind a metal desk on the factory floor, just like the older women, putting transistors and capacitors and resistors onto a computer board. Some of them were like strange small beans; shiny black and shiny brown. Some were like children's coloured toys, only far too small, of course — red and blue stripes on a kind of fawny colour. Some were tiny metal cylinders with thin legs. I followed the map and stuck the fiddly little things in the boards until tea-break, and then again until lunchtime, and then again until tea-break, and then again until home-time. It was a bit like doing a jigsaw. Sometimes I made mistakes because my mind would go off on a trip of its own. I tried not to make a hames of it.

'It's a good job and she was lucky to get it,' said Mrs Buckley in the shop to my mother.

There weren't many jobs around Atharnavar then. I tried my best, but sometimes a batch of them bloody boards would end up in the skip and it would be my fault and I would worry about losing my job and what they'd say at home. I'd be dreaming of him, you see. Sister Mary Regina said I wasn't bright but that I could surely hold down a job at Aces Factory if Mary Kelly could. Mary Kelly was fierce thick altogether, but she knew how to do the boards.

He was a hard case. He was an awful so an' so. He was a right chancer. That's what they said about him in the factory. But I thought he was the one for me. I got the thought into my head and couldn't get it out again, not even when I found out he had a wife.

'You're as handy as a small pot,' he said to me, when I made him a cup of tea at break-time. Most of the other women on the factory floor would tell him to 'eff off' and make his own tea.

'Don't encourage him, love,' said Mrs Mooney.

I liked making tea for him though. So I did.

Days came and days went. He sang a song about drinking buttermilk during the week and whiskey on a Sunday. He used to make my days feel like Sundays. It was work I looked forward to, not the weekends.

So here I am on the Tube train. I have a cleaning job in the hospital, on the night shift. While people like the smart couple opposite me are having after-work drinks or going to the theatre or to a fancy restaurant, I'm at work. I clean all night long, apart from two tea-breaks. It's okay so long as I don't have to talk to anyone. I don't mind cleaning, except for the Maternity Ward. I always feel sick when I'm on that, so I usually manage to get one of the other night-cleaning staff to swap with me.

That sick feeling. I hate it. I used to feel sick like that on Saturday nights at the Shamrock Ballroom, sick with worry that no one would ask me to dance. I'd sit along the wall in a row with the other girls, making pretend conversation, wondering inside my head why I bothered going to dances at all, desperate for some man to notice me. Then the girl sitting next to me would be asked up, and sometimes the girl on the other side as well, and I'd be the wallflower, sitting there like an óinseach, not knowing where to look.

Only the drunk lads who came in late and could hardly see me would ask me to dance. That fella who wore his Wellington boots, dance or no dance, used to nod me onto the floor. A girl from the town told me he wore nothing except his Wellingtons for so long that the skin between his toes had grown and his toes ended up all stuck together. The thought of that made me feel sick, but I didn't like to say no to him in case the other fellas thought I was a stuck-up bitch, and then no one else might ask me at all.

No more dances for me. My dancing days are over a long time now. I wish I could say the same about that sick feeling I get. Sometimes it doubles me over.

I opened my legs in the back of his Vauxhall Viva and let him do it. Let… him… do… it… Just like I laughed at his jokes and made him tea in the canteen and let him belittle me when he felt like it. I did that. I let him put his thing in me. He put his child seat in the boot of the car before we did it. It hurt.

I didn't tell anybody. How could I? Nobody said anything to me when I started getting big. *Nobody said a word.*

It hurt that night too. I was in agony when I went into the field in my nightie, no shoes, wet mud. I could feel one foot slide on warm cow dung. I was in pain. It came out. I hated it. His wife went to the hospital. I had to go out to the field. Hot tears, pain like a hot poker. I was an animal; that was all. The head came out. I pushed the rest out, held it hard around the neck, and shook it against the ground. I was mad at myself. It meant nothing to me. It was like a dead dog on a leash. I had to bite the stringy bit off or it would drag along the ground after me forever until I died. I bit it through. I hid it well.

All these long years later, I'm still scared. Some day, someone might find out.

I'm sitting here alone on this Tube train. No one here knows me. I wish I didn't know myself. Sometimes I dream about it. I dream I'm walking down Oxford Street, looking in the window of Boots, maybe, or Topshop, and the thing falls out of me and everybody in the street sees it dragging along behind me on the footpath on its fleshy string and I don't even notice. Then I see it trailing along behind me, slithering along the footpath like a big slug. I wake up with a terrible feeling that it's still there with me, that it's at the bottom of the bed. I have to scrabble down under the sheets to check. I shiver with cold and fear under the blankets. I'm not even relieved that it's not there, because it feels like it always will be.

HOLE IN THE BUCKET

It's 5.20 p.m. on a hot day in July and my head hurts. I'm about to slide out of the office through the side-door when someone calls my name. I've no choice but to slink back to the front desk, where Eva from Reception presides benevolently in crisp cotton and full make-up.

'I've got that number you asked for, Leanne,' she says. She comes out from behind her desk and hands me a folded piece of paper. 'I wrote down another number for you too, dear,' she adds, in a lower tone of voice. 'You know, when my marriage fell apart I was devastated. But I went to talk to somebody—her number's there—and, honestly, it did the world of good.'

'Oh. Thank you, Eva.' I take my diary out of my bag and place the paper carefully between two spare January pages. This is worrying. I only asked Eva if she knew a good electrician.

It's 5.32 p.m. and I'm going home on the rattling, oxygen-starved Piccadilly Line Tube. I can hardly breathe. I'd like to get out at the next stop, climb back up into the sticky city air, find an air-conditioned bar and order a nice cold beer, but I swore to myself this morning I wouldn't drink until the weekend. Since me and Killian split up three months ago, I've gotten into the habit of joining the Systems Support guys for after-work drinks every Friday, but lately the drinking seems to have extended itself to Mondays, Tuesdays and Wednesdays as well. There's no harm in it, but I probably should cut down a little.

Thing is, I like the company. I'm not shagging any of the lads, by the way. Wouldn't dream of it. They're just good friends. 'Don't shit on your own doorstep,' is what Killian, my ex, used to say. Pity he didn't take his own advice. I did try to be promiscuous myself after we split up, but I'm no good at it. I've decided I'm better off being celibate.

Alcohol is different. I'm not going to give that up. I overdid it a bit last night, that's all. Edward Barker, Freddie Megabyte, Loopy Goldsmith and myself went to the Shakespeare Lounge after work and played pool for hours, fuelled only by lager, Walkers crisps and pork scratchings. All three of them walked me to the Tube at closing time and I felt fine until I got out at Turnpike Lane, when my balance seemed to desert me. I had to crawl up the escalator on my hands and knees — but I got home all right in the end.

Eva from Reception couldn't possibly know about last night, could she? Why the hell did she give me the number of a therapist? It's a bit condescending, actually. I know I'm not one hundred percent but I'm coping well, all things considered. Okay, I did get a warning for bad time-keeping but I've improved a lot in the past two weeks.

Except for this morning. Blame the hot weather. I decided to wear a dress, but when I put it on I realised to my horror that my legs were like a cat's, so I had to shave them. Then I nicked my heel with a Ladyshave and blood began to dribble everywhere. I had to put a wad of toilet paper between the raw stripe on my heel and the back of my shoe, then I limped to the corner shop to buy bandages before getting the Tube to work. I was twenty minutes late, but I'd have been early only for that.

The Tube train is almost full and I feel 'dog-rough', as my Dad used to say. The smells of sweat and aftershave make me feel faint. Thank goodness I got a seat. A busker is singing at the other end of the carriage. She's not much good.

> *There's a hole in the bucket, dear Liza, dear Liza.*
> *There's a hole in the bucket, dear Liza, a hole.*

The man sitting next to me stands up and as he moves away I notice two singed circles on the velour seat covering. They remind me of the cigarette burns on my shabby green couch. I really must quit falling asleep in front of the television.

> *Then fix it, dear Henry, dear Henry, dear Henry.*
> *Then fix it, dear Henry, dear Henry, fix it.*

The singing voice is thin and definitely off-key.

> *With what shall I fix it, dear Liza, dear Liza?*
> *With what shall I fix it, dear Liza, with what?*

I wonder if I could get something in Homebase to fix the faulty sockets in the kitchen. Surely I wouldn't electrocute myself? I can't afford an electrician. I'm into my credit zone already and pay-day's not for ages.

'It's ridiculous to have only one socket that works,' I said to Killian a million times. 'I have to plug the kettle in to make tea first, then unplug the kettle to make toast. Normal people in normal kitchens don't do that.'

'It's simple to fix. Those electricians cost the earth,' he told me. 'I'll get round to it.' Of course, he never did.

> *With straw, dear Henry, dear Henry, dear Henry.*
> *With straw, dear Henry, dear Henry, with straw.*

The busker's voice sounds oddly familiar. I lean forward in my seat and glimpse her through the crowd of passengers standing in the aisle at the far end of the carriage. She's wearing faded black jeans and a long-sleeved grey t-shirt. Long dark hair hides her face and she continues to sing as she holds a battered hat towards the passengers nearest to her. Oh Jesus! She's asking for money — and I know her. It's Alicia. And she's practically begging.

> *The straw is too long, dear Liza, dear Liza.*
> *The straw is too long, dear Liza, too long.*

She's going to see me in a minute. What'll I do? Will I put my head down? Look at my shoes? Pretend I'm not here? She'll be embarrassed. I'll be embarrassed. She won't want me to see her like this, surely.

She moves robotically along the carriage as she continues to sing. Most of the passengers pretend she doesn't exist. They read books and newspapers, listen to their iPods and text on their mobile phones. Some of them shake their heads. A grey-suited man waves her away dismissively. A large lady counts her small change.

> *Then cut it, dear Henry, dear Henry, dear Henry.*
> *Then cut it, dear Henry, dear Henry, cut it.*

I put my hand in my bag and find my purse in one of the zipped compartments. I look inside it, furtively: two tenners and a few coins. I wonder how much I should give her. For a moment I contemplate getting off at the next stop before she notices me, but instead I sling the strap of my bag round my neck and stand up. As the train bucks and sways I make my way towards her, gripping one overhead handle after another as I lurch past seated passengers.

'Hi Alicia,' I say when I get closer. 'Long time no see!'

In the aisle I hang onto one of the central poles and smile as if we're home for Christmas and we've met by chance down the pub, but it must be six years, maybe eight, since that's happened.

'Hi,' she says. She seems only vaguely surprised to see me.

'How are you?'

'I'm okay,' she says.

Her face is very pale and there's a scar on her chin. A dark red stripe of lip-liner outlines the edges of her lips, but the lips themselves are colourless; she must have forgotten to put her lipstick on. I hate myself for noticing. I remember an afternoon in her house, before she dropped out of her beautician's course, when she gave me a facial, then a make-up lesson. She taught me a handy hint: *Use lip-liner around the edge of the mouth, then fill it in with lipstick, either a darker colour or a lighter colour, depending on whether you want to make your big lips small or your small lips big.* I was impressed.

'I knew you were in London — but it's amazing how easy it is to lose track of people, isn't it? I haven't seen Paula or Katy for years.'

'Me neither,' she says. Her eyes tell me nothing.

The train lurches to a halt at Caledonian Road and we both clutch the pole nearest to us.

'Mind... the gap,' says a disdainful male voice over the tannoy.

As people leave the carriage and others board, I try not to study Alicia too closely. I'm relieved her t-shirt has long sleeves. Maybe that talk about her being on drugs is rubbish.

'Are you still with Killian?' Alicia asks me after the doors close and the train moves on.

'No. No, I'm not.'

'What happened? You were together such a long time.' She looks at me sympathetically.

I swallow hard and try not to cry. 'I kicked him out a while back. He... well, he was unreliable.'

'All men are the same,' she says. 'My Dave... he's done a lot of bad things. But I love him, you know?'

'That's all very well...'

'I can't believe you split up with Killian. Everyone thought you were made for each other.' She looks at me with her big black eyes.

I don't want her to say any more. It hurts.

The train rolls into Holloway Road Station and screeches to a halt. People jostle on and off the train.

'I'm getting off at Finsbury Park,' she says.

'Me too.' I'm not too sure why I say this but actually it's a good idea. I'll get the bus to Crouch End, buy some food there, maybe a few cans of Red Stripe.

The doors close and I smell fried food with a hint of engine oil. I'm reminded of a summer back home… carnival smells of chips and candy floss, diesel and patchouli oil, chair-o-planes, roundabouts, bumper cars and the Big Wheel, hot sticky nights down town, spotting 'talent' with Alicia and the others.

'Do you remember Perks Fun Fair?' I shout, over the clanking noise of the train as it rushes through the tunnel.

'God, yes.' She seems animated all of a sudden.

'You ran away with the bloke who worked on the bumpers.' I can see him now, in my head. Emaciated rock-star thin; we mistook it for glamour. You could see his knees through his worn jeans. His hair was oily and black like the grease under his fingernails, and he leapt carelessly on and off the backs of the bumper cars with a fag in his hand and sparks in his hair, smiling at Alicia with a glint of gold.

'My mother went completely over the top,' Alicia shouts, above the noise.

'You were only fifteen, to be fair. She rang the police, didn't she?'

'Talk about ridiculous.'

The train stops abruptly at Arsenal and we're separated briefly as people disembark and others shuffle their way on. When the train sets off again, Alicia leans closer so that I can hear.

'They got the doctor for me and everything. We'd only gone up to his place in Sligo for the weekend. His mother wouldn't let me stay. I didn't want to, anyhow. You had to take your shoes off at the door and go outside to smoke. I thought he had his own place.'

It's noisy as the train rolls into Finsbury Park. Alicia steps off the train and onto the platform. I follow her as she makes her way through the crowd towards an exit. Her hair is still long but it's tangled. She used to iron it straight, back in the old days, on her mother's ironing board. Her mother nagged that she'd do herself damage and asked me to talk some sense into her, while Alicia said, 'Help me, will you? I can't do it all on my own.'

I'm not sure that Alicia wants to talk to me any more but I feel reluctant to let her go.

'Do you live near here?'

'Yeah.' She steps on the escalator and I follow. As we ascend, she adds, 'Sorry I can't invite you back for a cup of tea. The place is a mess at the moment.'

'So is mine. My mother would kill me if she saw the state of it.'

She says nothing.

'I was sorry to hear about your mother,' I add, quickly. 'I hope you got my card. I couldn't get home for the funeral. It was too late by the time I heard.'

'That's all right,' she says. 'Thanks anyway. She thought the sun shone out of your arse, didn't she?'

'I don't know where she got that idea.'

'She had a lot of strange ideas.'

I can't think of anything to say to that, so I say nothing.

At the top of the escalator Alicia walks through an open barrier, while I use my season ticket.

'I'm going this way,' she says when I catch up with her, indicating the right-hand tunnel.

'Me too.'

We walk on, towards the exit. A shaft of sun falls sideways along the floor just inside the tunnel and in the brightness she seems to fade.

'Do you fancy coming out for dinner some night? A few drinks?' I ask. 'It'd be my treat.'

She stops and squints in the sunlight of the street, pushing a swathe of dark hair behind one ear. Her skin does not look good in this light.

'Fine,' she says.

'Will I ring you?'

'Okay.'

I rummage in my bag to find my mobile phone, and then tap her number into my contacts list. 'Speak to you soon.' I hug her quickly, and walk round the corner to the bus stop. As I stand there, waiting for the bus, a terrible worry about Alicia overwhelms me. I take the two notes out of my purse — two tens — and run back the way I came, in time to see Alicia stub out a cigarette and walk into the Tube station.

'Alicia,' I shout. 'Wait a minute!'

She turns.

'A present.' I hold the money out. 'I've missed heaps of your birthdays.'

She stares at me, and her expression changes from surprise to a kind of hate. She grabs the two notes and shoves them in her jeans pocket.

'You have no idea,' she hisses. 'No fucking idea at all. You never had. Why would you, with your proper job and your proper boyfriends and your proper this and your proper that? Little Miss *fucking* Perfect.'

I stand in shock as she walks away. Then I run after her. She pushes through the crowd and steps onto the down escalator and I see the top of her head and then she's disappeared. I try to follow in her wake but the ticket collector stops me and asks to see my ticket, and by the time I reach the southbound platform she's not there. I try the northbound platform but she's not there either.

The back of my shoe chafes against my bandaged heel as I limp home. I smoke three Marlboro Lights on the way, to distract myself from the pain.

When I get home, I kick my shoes off, throw my bag on the floor next to them and slump down on the singed green couch. What the hell is wrong with Alicia? I was only trying to help. I ring the number she gave me. A puzzled male with very little English answers.

'Sorry, wrong number,' I say.

I'd kill for a drink now, but in all the upset I forgot to buy alcohol, or even food. There's a half-eaten Thai takeaway on the coffee table that's two, or maybe three, days old. The ashtray is overflowing and empty cans of Red Stripe lie helpless on the carpet, like skittles. Everything's a mess.

I drag myself up from the couch and walk barefoot into the bathroom. It shocks me, to be honest. It's in a right state after my shaving 'accident' this morning.

My stomach is rumbling, so I brave the kitchen where I locate a pot noodle that's only slightly out of date. I fill the kettle and unplug the toaster so that I can plug the kettle in and that's when I get a really weird, creepy feeling, as if I've been watching a version of myself doing this very same thing over and over again for a very long time.

'Ridiculous,' I say out loud, but I feel a bit shook by the events of the day. The pot noodle is disgusting. I look in the fridge for something else to eat. Lo and behold! There are two cans of Red Stripe glistening behind a hardened slab of yellowed cheddar cheese and a pot of jam. I'll just have one, I tell myself. I take it out, pluck the ring-pull off and drink from the can — and it tastes pretty fine.

While I pop open the second lager, I think about ringing the numbers Eva gave me, but it's too late to call anyone now. I'll clean up, instead, as soon as I've drunk this.

THE FOX AND THE PLACENTA

Marilyn sighs. 'I used to be such a fun-time girl.'

Unlike Monroe, this Marilyn is not a blonde. Her hair is russet-red and curly and right now her fun-time girl-self is hampered by the fact that she's nine months pregnant. She's sitting Humpty-Dumpty style on a green corduroy beanbag, watching Richard and Judy on the telly.

'I'm going out to get a better hose for the birthing pool,' says Brendan in his soft Derry accent. 'Will I get you a wee cake or something while I'm out?'

'Yes, please,' says Marilyn. Her sweet tooth has gone demented since the second trimester. 'Can I have some Clarnico Iced Caramels— you know the ones I mean? They're pink and white with toffee inside.'

'I think so.'

'If you see any, will you buy me a packet?'

'I will. Now ring me if you get a twinge — I'll come straight back.'

'Okay. I hope I won't have any more of those fake ones though. All pain, no gain. I'm fed up with them. What are they called again?'

'Braxton Hicks,' he says.

Top marks. He's read Miriam what's-her-name's *Parent and Child* book from cover to cover as if fatherhood is some kind of weird A-level. As if he's definitely the father. She's told him there's a chance he's not. He seems so sure it's his though.

'I think I'll go to bed for a while,' she says. 'I just can't get comfortable on this.' It's a huge struggle to half-roll, half-grapple her way out of the beanbag and onto her hands and knees. From this position she grabs the top rail of the birthing pool and hauls herself upright.

'Is this pool supposed to be full?' she says.

'No, no... I'll empty it before I go. I was just assessing the time it took to fill.'

'Thanks so much, Brendan. I really appreciate it. Gosh, I'm exhausted. Those bleeding foxes were howling again last night and between them and this,' she indicates her huge frontal bump, 'I didn't get a wink of sleep.'

She shoves her feet into her Birkenstocks and makes a slow journey to the bedroom. A pair of red patent high-heeled shoes from the January sales sit unworn on the shelf. She looks at them, sadly, before hauling herself onto the bed.

Nine months ago, everything was different.

Brendan was just her friend. Not a bit like her ex-boyfriend, Sam the love rat. As her friend Laura pointed out, Sam was mean and egotistical and Marilyn's better off without him.

'Brendan's much nicer,' said Laura. 'He's mad about you. But you can't resist bastards, that's your problem.'

'I'm not stupid,' protested Marilyn. 'I know Brendan's great. I've always loved him—as a friend, I mean.'

'Admit it, you can't allow yourself to fall for him because he's such a nice bloke.'

'It's just... he's not a hunter-forager-gatherer-you-Tarzan-me-Jane geezer, is he?'

'You'll never learn,' sighed Laura.

Nine months ago, Marilyn was at a loose end, still mourning the end of her relationship with Sam, when she found herself crying on Brendan's shoulder after an alcohol-fuelled night out. Every cliché in the book applies to the situation that followed. Herself a mess, Brendan declaring himself to be in love with her; throes of drunken passion, then waking with a fearsome hangover on a grey January morning, trying to remember what had happened. And Brendan lying there beside her in bed, like a fond dog. He, of course, remembered everything.

'I'll phone you later,' said Brendan, happily, at about midday. 'I've got to do some work but I'll ring you at six, okay?'

Sam called round that lunchtime to say he'd made a terrible mistake. Marilyn was only just out of the shower. As she pointed out to Laura afterwards, it's all very entertaining on TV but not when it happens to you.

'I was vulnerable,' she said. 'You'd be surprised how confusing things can be, especially when you have that hangover lust going on.'

When Sam left, having rid himself of 10cc (the sperm, not the 80s band), she knew she'd made a terrible mistake.

At 6 p.m. sharp, the phone rang.

'Hi,' Brendan spoke shyly. 'Are you okay?'

'Yeah. Why wouldn't I be?'

'Would you like to come out for dinner tonight?'

'Well,' she thought for a moment. 'Dinner? Where?'

'Well, I've booked Le Petit Prince. It's a new French-Moroccan place.'

'Oh.'

'But I can book somewhere else... whatever you like.'

'Oh no. That's... fine. What time?'

He arrived with flowers and paid for dinner, though she earned as much money as he did, if not more, and suggested more than once they should go Dutch. Good old Brendan. She wished she'd never been taken in, that last time, by Sam.

Marilyn lies back, bolstered by every pillow in the house, eyes closed, listening to the soothing music of Deep Forest. She feels like an over-blown balloon, ready to explode. She breathes in and out just like the yoga teacher at the Natural Centre for Birth and Rebirthing has taught her. She tries to soften each part of her body from the tips of her fingers and the top of her scalp right down to the soles of her feet. The 'Corpse Pose' it's called. Not such a nice thought. When you're pregnant, you want everything to be fertile and alive, not dead. There's another name for it too, Sumatra, something like that. No, Sumatra's a volcano, isn't it? The Corpse Pose. Funny the way she's practically devouring murder mysteries while waiting for the baby. Weird, that. Sam would have scorned such lowly literature... Sam's lying low for a while. His reaction to the little problem she's given him has not been great... The mystery of the double dads... Nothing like this happens in Agatha Christie books... Dead bodies in libraries... Caribbean mysteries...

A dog begins to bark outside. Maybe it's one of the foxes, but the foxes usually emerge only at dusk and their bark is almost a whine. Long rangy dog-like beasts, they're more like wolves than foxes.

More barking. She's determined to relax. *I'm going to sodding well relax if it kills me.* But she's distracted... Brendan has a cute face, like a friendly terrier. Sam is a wilder fox-type, tough, skinny, cynical. Behind the Victorian houses that form the lines of the Haringey Ladder, the foxes look more grey than red as they slouch in the shadows between street lamps. They're red foxes nonetheless. Mr Singh from Number Five has told her there are no grey foxes in England, that grey foxes live in North America. Maybe the London foxes have cross-bred with stray dogs. Now there are hordes of them, packs that come out when daylight turns to night. They roam through back gardens, foraging in people's dustbins, skulking near the kebab shop on Green Lanes, making forays on greaseproof paper packages, licking polystyrene trays outside the chipper. In her darkest nights Marilyn dreams of werewolves leaping for her throat, but most of the time she dreams of nothing.

Now she hears the key clicking in the front door. Someone shuffles in. There's the flapping of paper bags and footsteps going back in the direction of the kitchen. She fancies a cup of tea but it takes a while to manoeuvre herself out of bed. She stands up eventually and makes her way slowly downstairs.

Brendan's put the kettle on.

'Hi,' he says. 'How're you feeling?'

'Alright. Bored.'

'Will I make tea?'

'Yes, please.'

'I'd be back ages ago only I met Mr Singh — you know him — the old man in Number Five. He was in a chatty mood, told me they're selling dustbins in Wood Green Shopping Centre with a sign above them saying "Fox-proof". He's just bought one.'

'What does "Fox-proof" mean?'

'There's a special locking mechanism, apparently. He says the foxes are using teamwork to knock over the normal bins, even the big ones. I thought your bin had blown over in the wind, but Mr Singh says it's the foxes.'

'Did you get cake?'

'Not *just* cake.' He shakes a packet of Clarnico Iced Caramels in front of her.

'Great. I'll be like a mountain after the baby's born, but what the hell.' She can't wait to get her teeth into a pink Iced Caramel. As she chews, she wonders if this means the baby will be a girl. She's always wanted a little baby, though not quite like this.

Everything happens so fast.

'I think it's not a false alarm this time,' says Marilyn.

Brendan times the contractions, rings the Home Birth Team and fills the birthing pool at record-breaking speed with the new improved hose he bought earlier.

Marilyn's waters break in the birthing pool. She can't bear to stay in it a second longer. The midwife from Derry arrives to run the show and chats to Brendan about their favourite pubs in Magherafelt, while he covers the carpet with the towelling material he's bought.

'You're doing great, Marilyn,' says the midwife. 'Wonderful! You're five centimetres dilated already.'

The midwife from China arrives to administer rescue remedy and tiny homeopathic tablets to everyone, especially Brendan. The midwife from Derry thinks Brendan should have some brandy as well, so he does.

Marilyn walks naked in a cowboy mode around the room. She stops and groans sometimes and seems unaware of company.

'I'll sing,' Brendan says. He begins to sing 'I'm coming out' by Pink, but his voice is badly off-key.

'Shut up!' screams Marilyn and she shrieks for the TENS machine but soon she's too busy to bother with it. She holds Brendan's hand until he moans. The midwife from Derry tells Brendan he should have a break so he leaves the room to gulp more brandy in the kitchen, but he's back within minutes.

Marilyn is hanging off the radiator in the front room, then she's half-lying, half-squatting, on the floor.

'We've got to shout this baby out,' says the midwife from Derry to the midwife from China. 'Brendan, you support her on this side. Ling, will you hold her on the other? I'll stay in front.'

All four of them shout and count and breathe and yell 'PUSH!' when the midwife from Derry says 'Now'. Marilyn shouts loudest and the baby comes out. There is an enormous and blessed silence.

Brendan holds the baby for a moment before the midwife from Derry lays the child on Marilyn's breast. Marilyn looks at her baby and astounds herself by falling into a new kind of love. The baby makes its first mewling cry and somebody remembers to ask what sex it is.

Then the midwife from Derry tends to Marilyn and gives her an injection so the placenta will come out faster, and the midwife from China checks the baby (it's a boy) and the placenta comes out and Marilyn yelps while the midwife from China stitches her up and the midwife from Derry says, 'You won't remember half of this, you know,' and Brendan says, '*I* will. I'll never forget it. You were *wonderful*, Marilyn. You were amazing. You were mighty. You were an *Amazon*. I love you so much...'

It's ten hours since the baby was born. Marilyn lies back, eyes closed, determined to relax. The... what is it again? The Corpse Pose. Sumatra. Something like that.

The painkillers are beginning to wear off. Her stitches feel itchy and uncomfortable.

A dog barks. 'Oh God,' she groans quietly. 'Shut up.' More high-pitched whining and some clanking and banging noises out back. The sound of something falling. Brendan cursing.

The baby in the Moses basket beside her begins to cry. Marilyn wants to cry too. What on earth is she going to do? This tiny scrap of a thing needs a decent mother — one that knows how to breastfeed — one that knows who the father is.

Terrible noises out back. Is that Brendan roaring? More whines and clattering sounds.

She picks up the crying baby as if he's a Ming vase, careful to support his neck. She does everything in slow motion.

'Oh my poor sweet thing,' she says.

The baby stops crying and looks up at her with blind newborn eyes. She walks round the room with the child, talking gently.

'What's wrong with you? Why don't you go to sleep like a good little boy?'

She carries the baby downstairs. It's painful to walk. As she enters the kitchen she feels a cold breeze. The back door is open and rain is pouring down outside. Before she has a chance to close it, Brendan comes stalking in. He looks like a wild man, wet and sweaty at the same time. The knees of his jeans and the front of his sweater are muddy, as if he's been dragged through a swamp.

'Jesus!' he says. He's holding her biggest cooking pot. 'The fucking foxes knocked over the dustbin and one of them tried to make off with the placenta.'

'What?'

Brendan kicks the back door shut.

'It's okay, I got it back.' He holds out the cooking pot. It's filled with a huge fleshy thing that looks rank.

'Ugh, that's disgusting.'

'Nah. It's just natural. Don't worry, I'll give it a rinse. The thing is…'

'Oh God, why did you…?'

'Well, you were wrecked after giving birth so I didn't want to bother you. The midwife said some people like to bury the placenta in the garden and plant a tree.'

'Crikey, was all that inside *me*?'

'Yeah. So anyway… I wrapped it in a few bin bags and I put it in the dustbin before the midwife left. I was a bit dazed myself so I figured it would be alright there for a while.'

'And…?'

'Well, just now I heard the bin go over, so I ran out. There was a whole gang of foxes out there and one of them had the bag in his mouth.'

'What?'

'So I had to grapple with the fucker. Jesus, was I scared or what… I looked him in the eye and I swear to God he wanted that placenta as much as I did. We knocked over your garden bench, but it's okay, I can fix that…. Anyway, the rubbish bags tore and the placenta fell on the ground so I had to grab it before he had a chance to run off with it. It's grand though. There's only a couple of bite marks.'

'I don't even *want* the thing,' she says. 'I can't bear to look at it... It's so... revolting.' Marilyn sees disappointment in his face. 'Are you okay?' she adds.

'Grand. One of the foxes isn't so good, though.'

'Why?'

'I knocked him out. He's stretched out flat on the grass at the moment. I might have to call a vet.'

He beams at her as she shakes with laughter.

'No way I was letting some thieving fox go off with *your* placenta, kid,' he grins at the baby.

'Oh, oh, oh, my stitches,' she says. She's on the verge of wetting herself and it hurts to laugh so she stops.

'Gosh,' she says. 'You Tarzan, me Jane.'

'All part of the service.'

She stares at Brendan. There's a tough, lean, wild determination about him now. She looks down at the baby in her arms to see if there's a resemblance but the baby's just a small alien with a strange conical head. There's only a tiny bit of hair on it and it's red like hers; he's a little red fox. But the mouth, the mouth... surely that's Brendan's upper lip?

'You know,' she says. 'We have to arrange a paternity test as soon as we can.'

'I know that. I didn't want to talk about it though. Not till I had to.'

In the silence that follows, Marilyn remembers the moment after giving birth, when Brendan said he loved her. She thinks how easy, how nice, how convenient it would be if she could just tell him that she loves him too. She realises that's what she wants to say.

Marilyn looks through the back window. The rain has stopped now, and the sun is setting in an orange-red glow beyond the row of houses in the street behind hers. The sky is dark, almost purple, and she can barely see the shadows of the rooftops. No stars can be seen but she makes a wish anyhow.

'Brendan,' she says. 'Thank you for being so good to me. I can't think how you've put up with all this...'

'It's been difficult,' says Brendan. 'But you didn't lie, Marilyn. You're honest. And brave.'

Marilyn feels weak and teary. 'You're brave too.'

Brendan takes off his muddy sweater and throws it on the floor, before putting his arms gently around Marilyn and the baby.

'So,' he says. 'What are we going to call the baby?'

Marilyn closes her eyes and relaxes, and when she opens them again, she sees a fox walking wearily across the garden, disappearing into the night.

SALVAGE

I thought there'd be plenty of cheap bedsits to rent in Cork, especially these days, but I've seen four today, and they were all kips. My back is aching, my throat hurts and the thought of sleeping in the car for a third night is unbearable.

The fifth on my list is on the ground floor of a three-storey Victorian house, near the city centre. The place looks okay from outside, so I ease my Volkswagen Touareg into a parking space and hope for the best.

The woman who opens the door is about my own age, late thirties.

'Vincent, is it?' she asks. 'Come in. I'm Dolores.'

In the hall, a huge and furry white cat stares at me brazenly.

'I hope you don't mind cats,' Dolores says. 'This is Mao Zedong.'

'Mowsee-what?'

'Mao Zedong. I named him after Chairman Mao, leader of the Chinese revolution.'

'Ah, I see. Great name.'

She leads me along the hallway and unlocks a door.

'Stay out there, Mao,' she says.

The bedsit was once two rooms, she explains. She had the conversion done eighteen months ago, after her divorce. The furniture is modern—probably IKEA. There's a kitchenette and sitting/dining area to the left and a bedroom area on the right, near a big window that looks out on the back garden. The place is clean and smells of fresh paint.

I tentatively slide a kitchen drawer open and shut.

'Very nice,' I say.

The bathroom is across the hallway and though it's a botch job, it's not the worst I've seen today.

The cat reappears and hurls its furry bulk through the immense cat flap in the back door. The cat flap thuds back and forth before it gradually pendulums to a halt. The sound grates on my nerves. As I retreat I almost trip over a bowl of cat food. Then I notice the cat bed and litter tray under the stairwell.

Dolores hesitates, then explains, 'Mao likes to sleep down here— but he's no trouble.'

'Fine, fine. Do you have internet access?'

She does. The rent's reasonable. I'm surprised at how easy it is to bargain her down.

'I need to move in straight away.'

Dolores looks doubtful. 'Well, I usually need references.'

'I can give you a cash deposit and a cheque for the first month's rent.' I try not to sound stressed.

'I'm not sure,' she says.

'I'm only just separated from my wife, so would a phone call do? Here's the number of my ex-boss, Gus White, the Chief Fire Officer.'

'You're a fireman?' Her expression changes.

'Well, yeah, I used to be. I'm a fire safety consultant at the moment.'

'Wait here. I'll call him.'

Dolores returns.

'Gus thinks the world of you,' she smiles. 'He told me you got a medal for bravery when you worked in the Fire Service.'

'Oh.' Dim memories return: first on the scene, smoke, flames, an elderly lady with terror in her eyes, so light and fragile when I picked her up and carried her down a ladder to the waiting paramedics and the cheers of bystanders. 'Long time ago, now. Just part of the job.'

'That's not what Gus said. Come upstairs and we'll sign the agreement.'

Her sitting-room is comfortable; soft brown leather couches, a wood-burning stove. The cat's there now, dozing on one of the couches. Sky News is on the flat-screen television.

'Terrible what's been happening in Japan,' Dolores says. 'I'm glued to it. It's only getting worse.'

'Japan? I'm afraid I'm out of touch. And my car radio is on the blink...'

'It's horrific,' she says. 'Look — they're about to show it again.'

On the screen a wave is rolling in from the sea. At first, it seems like an ordinary wave as it surges towards some toys on a beach. It's not. It's a monster wave and the walls and buildings, houses, cars and boats that are being swept away are real. Real people, too, must be swirling in the mess of sea water and debris, their bodies churning hopelessly around and under.

'There was an earthquake first and that caused the tsunami,' she explains. 'They think the death toll will be more than 1,700.'

I stare at the screen while Dolores searches for keys. We sign a letting agreement, I give her a cash deposit and a cheque and thank her. My throat's like sandpaper. As I leave, the cat gives me the evil eye.

I drive back to Ballincollig, to the house I shared with Sheila, until last Wednesday. When we bought it, in 2007, the place seemed a bargain. Now it's in negative equity. Sheila's car, a cream-coloured Fiat 500, is parked in the driveway. I ring the doorbell instead of using my key, for fear of annoying her. She answers the door after a while. Though she seems tired and holds her dressing gown tight around her neck, she still looks beautiful to me.

'I'm knackered,' she says. 'I don't want to talk right now.'

'I just want to collect a few things.'

'Take what you want, then go.'

I leave the house with a bag of clothes, some bedding and my printer. I stop in Tesco for supplies: bread, cheese, milk, some ready meals, three bags of Taytos, a jumbo pack of salted peanuts, four bottles of cheap wine and a bottle of whiskey. Once Dolores cashes my cheque I'm pretty much skint, so I have to pay for the groceries on the joint credit card. Back in the flat, I'm annoyed at myself. I forgot to buy toilet paper and something for my sore throat. I don't have the energy to go out again, so I set up my laptop and printer instead. Bugger. I need a password for the internet. I ring Dolores.

'Come on up,' she says. 'I'll write it down for you.'

Her sitting room is warm and the news is on TV again.

'How are you settling in?' she asks.

'Grand. It looks like things are still dire in Japan?'

'Now they think there's some damage to a nuclear reactor,' she says. 'As if things weren't bad enough. You'd wonder why on earth anyone would build a nuclear reactor on a fault line.'

'The way people sow the seeds of their own destruction never ceases to amaze me.' I'm surprised at my own intensity.

When I met Sheila, she was studying medicine in UCC. She was blonde, gorgeous, brainy too. I fell for her big time. When she got an internship at a hospital in Edinburgh, she asked me to go with her. I'd have followed her anywhere. In Edinburgh I studied Fire Safety Engineering and worked nights in a pub. Soon, we were married, and when she got a job in Cork University Hospital, we moved back to Ireland.

That's when I set up Vulcan Fire Consultancy. For the first few years, I was so busy I practically lived in my car. I drove all over the country doing inspections, dashing off fire safety reports, working non-stop. The money was rolling in (at least four times a fireman's wage). Enough for holidays in Barbados, expensive clothes, top restaurants, jewellry for Sheila.

Now, though, builders have gone bankrupt, architects are on the dole, and the demand for fire safety reports is almost nil. I've little to show for it except my car. Sheila's been paying the mortgage and the bills for nearly two years and she's not happy about it. When she discovered — three days ago — that I'd run up a massive bill on the joint credit card, she went ballistic and asked me to leave. She wouldn't listen to any explanation, just said she wanted a divorce.

'It's symptomatic,' she said.

I asked her what she meant, but she wouldn't even look at me.

Back in the flat I log onto the internet, check my emails. Nothing from Sheila. Her last text said, 'Please stop ringing me and texting me,' so I email her instead to tell her I love her. I check her Facebook page to see if she's posted anything or changed her status. Nothing, thank God. My throat is really hurting now. I know I'm not supposed to ring Sheila but I do. No answer from the home number. I ring her mobile and *almost* leave a message on her voicemail saying I've got some kind of virus and need urgent medical advice.

I microwave a Tesco lasagne and drink half a bottle of the red wine. After the first glass it doesn't taste so rough. The latest news on the tsunami's not good. It looks like the nuclear reactor's banjaxed. I make up my bed and fall into it. I'm sure I have a temperature. It's too late to ask Dolores for a few Nurofen. I doze but can't sleep. Either the place is infested with rodents or Mao Zedong has mental health problems. For most of the night it prowls in the hall miaowing loudly and scratching at the skirting boards. At intervals it leaps in and out through the cat flap which thumps and flumphs and rat-at-ats back and forth.

At about 3 a.m. I stalk into the hall. The cat leaps through the cat flap before I manage to grab it. I inspect the cat flap and discover it can be locked, so I lock the cat out and set my alarm for 6 a.m. I'll get up and unlock it then. Dolores will be none the wiser.

At 3.20 a.m. I hear a loud thwack and a terrible yowl. I rush out and open the back door, hoping the damn cat hasn't broken its neck. The cat limps in, looking shocked. Guiltily, I tell the cat I'm sorry. It ignores me and consoles itself with cat food, miaowing pathetically between mouthfuls.

Next day I check my emails. All junk. I check Facebook. No change in Sheila's status. I watch BBC News on my computer. It's reckoned that in Japan the eventual death toll will be over 10,000. There's a problem with two nuclear reactors now. Youtube clips show people walking in mud through hills of debris that were once their homes. The places they lived in are unrecognisable. I wish I could feel more for those dazed, homeless people who can't even find the bodies of their dead, but the sorrow that I feel is mostly for myself. I don't know what to do, so I drive to Ballincollig again.

Sheila's Fiat is in the driveway. A dark blue Saab is parked on the road in front of the drive, blocking her car in. I ring the doorbell. Sheila takes ages to answer the door.

'Some bastard blocked you in there,' I observe, nodding towards the dark blue Saab.

'It doesn't matter. What are *you* doing here?'

'I need some files for work.' I feel exhausted and sick, but judging by the expression on Sheila's face, now is not the time to consult her about my sore throat.

'Okay, just get them and go.' She marches upstairs. There's the sound of a key turning in a lock.

In the utility room that also serves as my office, or did, before all the hassle began, I throw some files into a plastic bag. When I look around to check for anything else I might need, I notice the box that contains my medal, sitting dusty on a shelf, so I slip it in my pocket.

Outside, I turn and look up at the bedroom window. Sheila's there, drawing the curtains shut. It seems odd that all I can see now is the lining of those curtains, even though I know so well what they look like on the other side: velvet, the colour of a Golden Delicious apple. Sheila chose them because they matched the carpet. I remember a summer day, lying in bed with Sheila and watching the curtains sway just a little in the breeze from the open window.

As I head back to my car I walk past the blue Saab. That's when I notice a sticker on the front windscreen, which reads:

STAFF PARKING
CONSULTANTS' PRIVATE CLINIC
CORK UNIVERSITY HOSPITAL

Numbly, I put the bag in the boot. For a while I sit in the car, holding the steering wheel tight in both hands, going nowhere. I feel as if I'm submerged in deep, cold water, unable to breathe.

When I get back, Dolores is cleaning out the litter tray in the hall, while the cat lounges in its catbed.

'Hi,' says Dolores. 'How are things?' She looks anxious.

'Not bad,' I lie. 'How are you?'

'Terrible. Mao was really off-form this morning. The vet says he must've got into a fight.'

'Actually, I've had an awful day,' I admit. 'Would you like a drink?'

'I could do with one. Why don't you come up to my place?'

I bring up a bottle of wine and the jumbo pack of peanuts. Dolores pours two large glasses of wine. She sits too close and jokes that she never expected to live with a cat. I tell Dolores that my wife kicked me out only three days ago and she's already found someone else.

'I haven't even had the chance to tell anyone we've separated yet.'

'That's awful. "Shingling" is what it's called, you know.' Dolores fills our glasses again. 'My husband did the same thing. He was test-driving the slaggy bitch for a full year before I found out. He said he couldn't decide whether to leave me or dump her.'

I gulp my wine. Dolores opens a second bottle.

'The new wife wears so much fake tan she looks like an oompah loompah,' she adds. 'But I'm over it now.'

'All I want is for everything to go back to the way it was.'

She shakes her head. 'There's no going back. I used to wish there was. You've no choice but to go forward.'

I go down to my flat to get the whiskey, while Dolores makes toasted cheese sandwiches. Upstairs again, I pour two big glasses of whiskey, and tell Dolores I'm finding it hard to sleep at night because of the racket the cat makes.

'Yerrah, why don't you shove him into the downstairs bathroom if he's a nuisance?' she slurs. 'Sure, he'll be fine in there.'

Soon afterwards, she falls asleep on the couch.

Downstairs, I have a little difficulty in unlocking the door of my bedsit but I'm not totally wrecked because I actually remember to drink some water. I don't feel like sleeping yet so I turn on my laptop to check the latest news. A BBC World reporter looks out from the screen. She says that in the north of Japan, a wet snow has fallen on nearly half a million newly homeless people. The screen shows an elderly Japanese man searching in the snow. His face is lined and full of sorrow and his clothes seem flimsy. I wonder how on earth he'll find what he's looking for. The situation with the nuclear reactors sounds worse than ever. I watch scenes of the disaster over and over again. Whole towns and cities washed away, thousands dead or dying, all those Japanese people being swept away by that tsunami, their houses floating like bathtoys on the waves.

At about 4 a.m., I wake up. Mao's in the hall mewing and scratching at a skirting board. My mouth is dry, my throat is sore and my head is pounding. I stagger into the hall and unlock the bathroom door. I drink from the tap and take a piss. Back in the hall I slowly approach the damn cat.

'Puss, puss,' I cajole him. 'Here puss, puss.'

To my surprise the cat comes over, nudges his head against my hand and purrs. I grab him with both hands, launch him through the bathroom door and slam it shut.

In the morning I grope for some clothes and head across the hall to the bathroom. As I brush my teeth I hear a miaowing sound. I can't see the cat anywhere. I turn the tap off. There's no sound. I turn the tap back on, then off again. Mao miaouws. For a moment, I wonder if the cat has died and come back to haunt me. Then I realise the sound's coming from somewhere underneath the bath. Sure enough, there's a gap at the side of the bath where the wood panelling has rotted. It's at the end where the taps are. I peer into the hole. Something rustles. There's a sobbing kind of mewl.

'Here kitty, kitty, kitty, here Mao,' I whisper. 'Come on out.'

I put my hand into the hole and try to grab the cat, but he seems to be wedged somewhere at the back of the bath between the pipework and the wall. I have a vague recollection of someone, somewhere, explaining why cats find it difficult to go backwards. I tell Mao not to worry, and rush back to my place.

Armed with a knife and a metal ladle, I dash back to the bathroom and begin to lever the wood panelling off the side of the bathtub. As the wood splinters and the cat emits low and terrified wails I keep repeating, calmly, 'Don't worry. I'll save you.'

Finally, the hole is big enough. I stretch my arm in. At last, I'm able to grasp the cat. His body feels astonishingly fragile underneath the mass of fur as I ease him gently through the fractured wood.

I sit on the tiled floor of the bathroom and stroke the trembling cat.

'It's alright,' I tell him. 'You're safe now.'

Finally, he begins to purr.

Soon, I'll have to tell Dolores what's happened, but at least the cat's alright. I'll fix the damage somehow. I'll ask Gus if any jobs are coming up in the Fire Service. Even a part-time one would do. In the meantime I'll sign on. Somehow, I'll manage.

ESMÉ'S WEEKEND

FRIDAY 4 p.m.

Esmé is alone in the elevator, so she dances to the piped muzak, using her handbag as an imaginary dance partner. When the lift shudders, signalling its halt, she stops dancing and hurriedly puts her handbag down by her side. Ping. The lift door opens. She steps out. Whoosh. The lift door closes behind her.

The entrance hall is decorated in neutral shades of grey and beige, and as Esmé walks towards the door that leads to the street, she smiles at the older woman sitting behind the reception desk, who smiles back.

'You're leaving early then, Esmé?'

'I am indeed. I managed to send everything to the printers at three, so I'm off!'

'Lucky you. Have a good weekend.'

'You too, Stella. See you Monday!'

Esmé walks along Oxford Street and turns left towards Soho. She hums an old Irish song about days coming and days going, drinking buttermilk all the week, whiskey on a Sunday, for she's Irish, despite her name.

She's going to Azzopardi's Delicatessen to buy fresh pasta. It's not always easy to think of nice things to cook. Fergus, her partner of ten years, is a vegetarian. The smell of meat, cooked or raw, makes him want to throw up, he says, so she's happy to humour him, content to forgo the pleasures of meat at home. She makes do with an odd illicit bacon sandwich on an early morning market trip and an occasional aromatic chicken tikka masala in a cheap Indian restaurant. She doesn't go home to Ireland often these days, but she can still dream up the strong smell of lamb stew and the salty tang of bacon and cabbage. It's an effort to cook a tasty dish with beans and brown rice after a hard day at the office. Sometimes it seems like a penance. Today, though, it's going to be deliciously simple.

She walks down Wardour Street, past the topless bar where a thin, sad-eyed girl in black lace sits on a stool just inside the door. There's a hole in the girl's fishnet tights and her mascara is carelessly applied.

In Old Compton Street, outside the Blue Bar, men sit at high tables drinking coffee or small glasses of wine while they scan younger men in tight jeans. Farther on, outside Maldini's Café, Esmé's friend Larry sits alone, smoking a cigarette. Louis, he calls himself now. That's his new chat-up name.

'Hiya! Are you waiting for a date?'

'Hot one, love,' he says. 'At least, I hope so! Oh, I think that's him now. Phone you soon, yeah?'

'Okay. Good luck!' She smiles and walks on until she reaches the delicatessen.

Esmé loves Azzopardi's. It smells good; nothing like the city just outside its door. It smells of garlic, vinegar, olives, cheese and fresh-baked ciabatta. Veined sausages in net stockings hang rudely over the heads of the customers, along with garlic and chillies. Cardboard boxes of panettone are stacked, in order of size, behind the counter. Jars and tins of olives, artichokes, tomatoes, pickles and things she does not recognise sit on the shelves. There is a wall of wine. Complicated tins of biscuits with beautiful names make a pyramid on the floor: amaretti, quaresimole, canestrini, ciocchini. She longs for them, but she never brings sweet things home. Fergus has told her not to; he was a fat child, he says, and can't handle temptation.

She stands in line in front of the refrigerated glass display cases, and admires the fresh pasta sitting in small troughs. The white-coated shop assistants weigh ravioli and slice salami and pepperoni and snip generous bulbs of garlic from the strings hanging like Christmas decorations from the ceiling, and they chat all the while, sometimes in Italian.

Mr. Azzopardi recognises her.

'Buon giorno, Esmé,' he says.

'I've never been to Italy,' she says, cheerfully, as he takes her money at the till. 'I know I'll love it when I get there.'

Esmé boards the Tube train. It's not yet peak time, so she slumps with relief into a seat and puts her bags on the floor next to her feet.

The prosperous-looking man opposite her is reading *The Financial Times*. The pink pages are drooping over the thin man sitting next to him, who leans sideways, and looks distinctly pissed off, but says nothing.

Esmé glances at the front page headline, which reads: 'Chancellor's Positive Approach to Negative Equity'. *Yes*, thinks Esmé. *A positive approach. Think positive.*

It's hard to keep thinking positive. Fergus is often out of work and it eats into her earnings. She's tired of paying the mortgage and all the bills, tired of being upbeat when Fergus is feeling low.

She thinks about how proud she was when he got that scholarship to RADA eight years ago. They'd been going out together for two years. He'd dropped her before he moved to London, but after a few weeks he was ringing her at all hours and begging her to come over.

He couldn't live without her, he said. He was miserable. He couldn't cope. He was taking speed, and drinking far too much. She'd already begun to make plans of her own that didn't involve London, but she decided those plans could wait. She loved him.

She got a job as a clerical assistant on a life-style magazine and steadily progressed to become a senior editor. He was in occasional work and frequent despair until he got a bit-part on *Sixpenny Avenue* — a Channel 4 soap opera — three years ago. Fergus is so cynical about most things and she was amazed, but delighted, at how easily he fell into the role of 'celebrity'. He'd always ridiculed the speciousness of it all, but once he became a 'soap star' he reveled in it. He loved receiving fan letters, being chased by paparazzi, the flash of cameras as he came out of nightclubs, seeing his handsome face in tabloid newspapers. It was a shock when his character was written out of the script so soon. He had a mere twelve months of being famous, then one twist in the script meant that his character died a sudden death, and somehow the work had dried up ever since. But that's show business. Things will pick up, she always tells him. She wishes he could stop being so bitter, but he claims that everyone is against him.

Think positive, she tells herself. *Somebody has to.*

She enters the flat quietly. She's going to surprise Fergus. The door isn't double-locked, so she knows he's in. He's careful to lock up when he goes out.

She tiptoes into the hall.

The front room is empty.

The kitchen is empty.

She puts her head cautiously around the bathroom door, but he's not in there either.

She bursts into the bedroom, holding up her two white plastic bags.

'Ta daaaah!' she says.

She stops.

'Oh,' she pauses. 'Sorry.' Then, 'What are you doing?'

He looks sideways in surprise. He is alone, sitting on the edge of the bed with his jeans and Y-fronts pulled down around his ankles. Pieces of torn foil lie on the carpet next to his feet. He looks up. He's in the process of putting a condom on his erect penis. It is half-on, half-off, plastic drooping. Now he begins to droop too.

'I... I... I wasn't expecting you home so soon,' he stammers.

'I finished early,' she says. 'Look, I have some nice things for supper. Fresh pasta from Azzopardi's. A couple of nice bottles of white wine. One's got one of those baskets on it, so I can make the bottle into a lamp later...'

Silence.

'What the hell is going on?'

'I just — Ah, I just thought I'd try these out. I mean, it might be a good...'

'But I'm on the pill. I thought we agreed? I've been on the pill for years.'

'Well, exactly.' He suddenly seems surer of himself. 'It can't be good for you. I was thinking maybe it's time for you to stop taking it.'

'Oh. Well. I think I'll put these away, anyway,' she says. 'Give you a chance to, you know...'

She's putting the wine in the fridge when he comes into the kitchen,

'Sorry about that,' he says. 'I feel like a right dickhead. What did you get?'

'Oh, some olives stuffed with almonds, parmesan crisps, a salad with mozzarella and artichokes, some lovely ciabatta bread, tortelloni filled with spinach and ricotta cheese, and a freshly-made tomato and basil sauce. Plus the wine.'

'Can we afford all this?' he asks.

'Oh fuck it,' she says. 'It's only money.' *My money*, she thinks but doesn't say it. 'We might be dead tomorrow.'

They eat stuffed olives and parmesan crisps and they drink wine. Mozzarella and artichoke salad and more wine. Tortelloni in pools of tomato sauce, sandy with parmesan cheese. And more wine. He goes to the off-licence for more wine. They have sex on the nondescript carpet in a desperate kind of way.

'I love you,' she says.

'I love you too, more than anyone,' he says, as he pulls a rug from the couch and drapes it over them.

'Are you having an affair?' she asks. 'I'm really freaked out by that whole condom thing.'

'What? You must be joking,' he says.

'I need to know.'

'Don't be talking rubbish,' he says and kisses her on the cheek.

She turns her head to stare at the carpet she's lying on. 'I hate this carpet,' she says. 'Let's rip it up and throw it away.'

'We can't afford another one. We'll have to leave it for now.'

'We can sand the floorboards. I had a look. They seem okay. Anything is better than this old carpet.'

'We don't know what's underneath. Anyway, I don't have time at the moment.'

'I can do it myself.'

'We'll see.'

'I think I'll go to bed now,' she says.

'Me too.'

In bed, she sits, propped by pillows.

'I was popular,' she says. 'When I met you.'

'I know,' he says. 'You were going out with that guy, what was his name?'

'Michael. He was lovely. He wanted to marry me.'

'He had a photo of you. He showed it to a few of us in the pub. You were laughing and leaning against a wall with a cigarette in your hand. That's the first time I saw you.'

'All my friends wondered why I bothered with you. They thought I was crazy. You were so odd and so angry. When I saw you act, though, I knew you were amazing. I could see straight away you had talent.'

'Well, it's not so evident now, is it?' he says.

'I was so proud of you when you got that scholarship to RADA,' she says. 'And when you got the part in *Sixpenny Avenue* — that was brilliant. It was such a great role. I could never understand why they dropped you.'

'Yeah, well,' he says. 'I don't want to talk about it.'

She can't sleep for a long time. She wakes in the night when he shouts out in his sleep.

SATURDAY 8 a.m.

He gets up first. She can smell the burning toast a few seconds before she hears him cursing. She drags on her dressing gown.

'Good luck with the audition,' she says. 'Are we still going shopping this afternoon?'

'If you want to,' he says.

'I was planning to go to John Lewis. Just for a look round.'

'I'll meet you at one,' he says. 'At the latest. At Finsbury Park. Should be done by twelve anyway. It's only a bloody advert. Why the wankers can't hold auditions at a reasonable hour, I'll never know.'

He fumbles around, searching for clothes.

'I don't know what to wear,' he says.

'How about that white t-shirt I bought you? Under your leather jacket. Simple, but nice.'

'Oh, I don't know.'

'You've had all week to decide.'

After he leaves, she eats a boiled egg carefully, with lightly toasted bread and butter and a cup of pale tea.

'Go to work on an egg,' she says out loud. It was an advertising campaign once — people using eggs as cars, she thinks, vaguely.

Her mother had always made her eat an egg on an exam morning. Hardboiled. Good for the brain. She could hardly swallow it, just like now, but she forced herself. She had always tried to please her mother and make that look of dissatisfaction on her face go away, if only for a brief while.

Esmé's mother had admired elegant things: dark chocolate and delicate lace; handsome men with sculpted cheekbones who starred in American made-for-TV movies; strong coffee and croissants; fine wine and paté. She had not fancied cups of tea or glasses of Guinness or solid men with reliable hands or brown bread or red meat. She'd loved France and the French language, hence the name she'd given to her only child. She often said she must have been French in a previous existence, though somehow she only managed to get to Paris three times and she was already dying by the third trip. Life had been a disappointment to her mother. Not elegant at all. Even the design of her coffin would have been a let-down.

Esmé's father, on the other hand, is one of those solid men with reliable hands who could never be described as elegant, but he had somehow won her mother over, in an unimaginable far-away time before Esmé was born.

He's a butcher and works long hours in his butcher's shop, lugging carcasses out of the cold room, hacking and chopping, slicing and mincing, wrapping parcels of meat in neat brown paper parcels, tying them deftly with twine and a loop for carrying them, then handing them over the counter to his customers. He never asked Esmé's mother to lift a finger and has always washed his own bloodied aprons in the small sink of the butcher's shop.

He's a cheerful man despite being surrounded by dead meat. She remembers a time she'd been sent to the shop by her mother with instructions to collect some sliced ham. Atharnavar had won some match or other that day — maybe it was the County Final — she doesn't remember now. She waited politely while a handful of customers stood in pleased conversation about the match and her father smiled and agreed, chopped and parcelled. Then a man called Toddy Power, a notable GAA fanatic, rolled into the butcher's shop, all addled with drink and triumph. 'Up the 'Var!' he shouted and demanded something for his frying pan. 'Give me mate or I'll ate me mickey!' he roared happily, and Esmé's father laughed so much it took him a while to recover.

Why couldn't my mother laugh like that? Esmé wonders, remembering the lines of discontent on her mother's fine-boned face, and that air she had of having been cheated out of some other, more exotic life. Esmé sighs and throws the pieces of broken eggshell in the bin.

An old metal filing cabinet stands in a corner of the bedroom. Esmé found it in a junk shop and thought it was a bargain at twenty quid. She bought it before realising she had to pay another twenty quid to get it delivered. It was a putrid green so she painted it black, but the paint had run a bit in places and the drawers always stuck.

She and Fergus share it. One drawer is hers. It holds her curriculum vitae, passport, photographs, letters and papers keeping fond memories safe. Another drawer contains bank statements, mortgage and life assurance details, guarantees and receipts; all the practical, boring pieces of paper that accumulate over time. The other two drawers are his: for promotional videos, publicity photographs, scripts he's working on, his novel-in-progress, various things that are going to work out, one day. He's the creative one and he needs his space.

She wrestles with the bottom drawer and finally jams it open. Then she takes it completely off its runners, empties everything out, and sets to work. She has a bad feeling.

In Finsbury Park Tube station, Fergus and Esmé walk past a busker who's playing 'Take it Easy' by the Eagles on an out-of-tune guitar. There's an agonised expression on the busker's lined face as he caterwauls into the chorus.

'God, he's really murdering that song, isn't he?' says Fergus.

'Poor fucker,' she says. 'He's probably desperate for money.'

Fergus opens his mouth but says nothing.

They stand on the platform. She can see dust swirling in the air in the wake of the train they have just missed. Mice tiptoe between the rails. Another train clatters in. They get on. There's nowhere to sit, so they stand, holding onto a pole.

'What's up with you?' he says, as the train jangles along.

'Nothing. How was the audition?'

'Crap. The usual. They'd already decided to give the part to Jason.'

'Are you sure?'

'I'm sure. They're all dickheads.'

'I wish I had a car.'

'You know cars aren't environmentally sound.'

'Or a gun,' she adds, as the train screeches to a halt at Highbury and Islington.

'What?' he shouts above the noise.

'Nothing,' she says.

The doors open and they move aside to allow people to get out and others to board. The doors shut and the train moves off. Fergus jostles her gently. 'Hey,' he says, and takes one of her hands in his. He rubs the inside of her palm with his thumb in a way that has always mesmerised her.

'I remember the first time you chatted me up,' she says, sadly. She allows her hand to rest in his.

'I know. God, I followed you around all night at that party, trying to get you to notice me. I had to get drunk before I had the courage to make a move on you...'

'I noticed you then all right.'

The train jangles on.

'It seems a long time ago,' she says.

'Hey, look at that!' He points at an advert pasted above the Tube train window. 'There's going to be another season of that celebrity quiz. I should try to get onto that. Maybe that's what I should be doing. What do you think?'

Shoppers meander through a maze of cosmetic counters and jewellery displays on the ground floor of the John Lewis Department Store, where perfumes make the air heavy.

Esmé grips the escalator tightly on the way to the furniture department on the third floor. She often walks around this store making mental lists of what she'd like to buy. Usually she enjoys this, but today she feels faint and everything looks foggy.

'What's wrong?' Fergus asks. 'Are you sick?'

'I don't feel so good.'

She looks at coffee tables in a languid kind of way. She can't afford the table she likes most.

'When I'm working again,' he says. 'We'll get that.'

He writes down the make and the price on an old card he finds in his wallet.

'I need food,' she says. 'I feel weird. Like I can't eat but I need food.'

They go to the restaurant at the top of the building.

The smell of meatballs in sauce wafts out from the hot food section.

'That smell is disgusting,' he says.

'I'm fed up of being vegetarian,' she says, weakly. 'Comfort food, that's what I want. Meatballs or beef stew. Shepherd's pie. Even a few rashers would be fine.'

'I don't know how you can possibly want to eat crap like that,' he says. 'But please yourself.' He goes off to find the salad bar.

She shivers while she queues for beef goulash, but when she sits down to eat it she can hardly swallow.

'You don't seem well. We should leave soon,' he says, when he's finished his couscous salad.

'I want to go to the kitchen department first.'

He trails behind her as she wanders through corridors of fridges and washing machines, dishwashers and microwaves. She stares at food mixers and baking trays, juicers, coffee-makers, sewing machines, liquidisers. She studies rows of classic kitchenware: Le Creuset in honourable blue, in warm reddish orange, in an honest green; solid pots and pans for an imaginary kitchen she doesn't have. She considers cutlery with lifetime guarantees; plastic storage boxes in various shapes and sizes for things that you can put away, safe in the knowledge that they will still be there when you look for them again; children's lunch boxes with cartoon characters she doesn't recognise, for children she doesn't have. Esmé yearns for all these things now, and fears she'll never need them.

'I need knives,' she says.

'But we have knives,' he says.

'I don't mean ordinary knives.'

She looks at carving knives, bread knives, vegetable knives, paring knives, serious chefs' knives, Sabatier, Henckels, Kitchen Devils, rows and rows of knives.

'£25,' she reads on the label of a wooden block of knives. 'These are what I need.'

'Alright,' he says. 'I'll buy them for you'.

'You'll get them?' she says. 'But you don't have any money.'

'I'll get them,' he says, and he hugs her.

He carries the knives in a strong white plastic bag with green lettering. As they travel home he holds the bag in one hand and her hand in the other, occasionally rubbing the inside of her palm with his thumb, almost hypnotising her into believing that everything is the way she thought it was.

She takes out the block of knives and puts them on the kitchen counter.

'I need a drink,' she says. 'Go on, let's have a drink.'

'Okay,' he says.

He takes a bottle from the fridge and pours two glasses of cold white wine, then hesitates and says, 'If you're not feeling well, maybe you shouldn't drink.'

'It doesn't matter,' she says. 'I'll never feel well again.' She drinks half the wine, then puts her glass down carefully. 'You've been lying,' she says. 'You dirty bastard. I'm on the pill. Do you want to kill me, is that what you want?'

'What?' he says.

'I always respected your privacy,' she says.

'I've no idea...' he says.

'I always respected you,' she says.

He says nothing.

'What kind of fool am I?' she says.

He looks at his glass of wine.

'I went through your stuff. I never even dreamt of going through your stuff before. You've been writing fiction all right,' she says. 'The fan letters. Writing to the kind of crazy women who write fan letters. Having sex with women who write fan letters to someone they don't even know. Are you mad?'

'It's not what you think,' he says.

'I never knew. You told me you loved me.'

'I do love you. They were nothing,' he says. 'A mistake.'

'How many?' she says.

'I just... it's just... I didn't have much experience when I met you. They were just available.'

'Available? Just for experience? Are you insane? Just how much experience did you think you needed?'

'I never wanted to leave you, Esmé. You're the best. None of them came close to you.'

'You must be mad,' she says. 'So I'm the best, am I? I didn't realise I was in some kind of competition.'

'I love you,' he says. 'I can't do without you.' He backs against the kitchen counter and stares at her.

'I found your bank book too,' she says. 'What kind of fool am I? You have five grand I didn't know a thing about. Imagine... Five thousand pounds. And here I am with no savings at all.'

She cries silently. Tears run down her face.

'Ten years,' she says. 'Ten fucking years.'

'It was just sex,' he says. 'They meant nothing, really.'

'Jesus Christ,' she says. 'How many?'

'It meant nothing. It's you I love.'

'What were you doing with the condom?'

'Practising.'

'So it finally occurred to you that maybe you should use condoms with these people? You were practising how to use condoms so you could use one next time? You fucking bastard, did you not even think about the risks? Did you not even care that you might kill me?'

He says nothing.

'I suppose everybody knows,' she says. 'Everyone but me.'

SUNDAY 5 a.m.

Esmé wakes up. Her eyelids are almost stuck together with sandman tears. Her pillow is damp.

They are entwined in the bed, and she disengages herself slowly. He is asleep, twisted in the white sheets. Dark curls stick to his forehead. She looks at him, at his beautiful angular bones, before she slides out of bed.

A large white t-shirt lies on the floor next to the bed. 'Keep It Live' is written on the front in big red letters. She puts it on and leaves the room in her bare feet.

In the kitchen, moonlight slants across the white Formica worktop and casts a shadow beyond the block of knives. She draws out the largest knife. It's a bread knife. She puts it back. She draws out the next knife. This one is long and sharp and meant for meat. She holds the knife in one hand and feels the edge gently with the other. She stands on the cold linoleum and looks at the carving knife in the semi-dark, for what seems like a long time.

She walks back to the bedroom and looks at the sleeping man. She moves closer and holds the knife above him. He groans in his sleep.

'It's not real,' he mutters and then he turns over.

She doesn't move for a moment. Then she turns and walks back to the kitchen where she replaces the knife in its slot in the wooden block.

She finds the phone and dials a number. 'The Samaritans please,' she says. 'No, just the number.' She writes down the number. She dials and hears only a flat bleep. Engaged. She dials again. Engaged.

SUNDAY 10 a.m.

'You love yourself so much, and you hate yourself so much, that you can't see anybody except yourself,' says Esmé. 'And I'm a fool. I could never see anyone but you.'

'I'm going to change,' he says. 'I've got it all out of my system now.'

'Please leave,' she says.

'I'm not going anywhere. I've nowhere to go.'

'You have to leave.'

'Look, I'll get therapy. It's never going to happen again. We'll get married.'

'Get married,' she says. 'Ha ha. That would be funny if it wasn't so fucking sad.'

'I'm going nowhere,' he says. 'I made mistakes, but that's over now.'

SUNDAY 6 p.m.

Esmé wanders the streets and finds herself outside her friend Maire's house. She rings the bell and Maire opens the front door, wearing an apron. A smell of Sunday roast oozes from the kitchen and Esmé realises she's eaten hardly anything since Friday night.

Maire hugs her. 'We're just about to have dinner,' she says. 'Will you have some?'

At the kitchen table a plateful of chicken, roast potatoes, vegetables and gravy is set before Esmé and she eats too fast.

'Have some more,' offers Maire.

Esmé tears chicken wings off the carcass with her hands and rips small shreds of meat from the bones, while Maire's husband Carlo feeds spoonfuls of potato and gravy to their two-year-old daughter.

'I thought you were a veggie,' he says.

'Yeah. What's wrong?' asks Maire.

'Everything.'

MONDAY 9 a.m.

Esmé sits at the kitchen table and makes a phone call.

'I'm really sorry, I can't come in. I'm not well.'

There's a pause, then she replies. 'I may need a few days.'

She listens. 'Thank you,' she says.

MONDAY 10 a.m.

In the local butcher's shop, the rank scent of dead flesh and the clunking sound of the cleaver almost make her weep. The refrigerated display case is filled with pale chicken breasts, beef steak, lamb chops and pork loin all lined up in neat rows next to containers full of mince, slick-looking livers and skinned chicken thighs. She recognises the real world behind the display; the world of her father, of the cold room and carcasses, of skin and bone, lard and gristle, veins and sinews, flesh and blood.

'I need lots of meat,' she tells the butcher. He listens, then hacks and slices and trims the meat she's asked for. To her disappointment he puts the meat into separate plastic bags; he doesn't package them neatly and tie them up with butcher's twine as her father does, back home.

'I'd like some chicken livers too,' she adds. 'And a lamb's heart.'

Back at the flat, she puts the bags on her kitchen counter and switches the oven on at gas mark 6. She places a joint of bacon carefully in a saucepan of water and fires up the gas ring underneath it. Next, she puts a leg of lamb on a greased roasting tin and slides it into the oven. She heats the frying pan until it sizzles, then covers its Teflon surface with streaky rashers. She shakes a wok, half-filled with chicken livers. She turns rashers with a fork. The kitchen air soaks up a miasma of greasy steam and meaty smells. The block of knives sits in readiness, next to a plate of uncooked sausages.

Fergus comes into the kitchen. There's a horrified expression on his face.

'What are you doing?' he says. 'It's disgusting. The whole place is stinking.'

'What?' she says. 'I can't hear you. I'm busy.' She stabs each pale pink sausage with a fork, then flings them roughly, one by one, into the pan where they splash, then sizzle alongside the rashers.

'I feel sick.'

'Get out. Your bags are packed. They're in the hall.'

'You must be joking,' he protests.

She uses a soup ladle to scoop some half-cooked chicken livers out of the wok. Then she throws them at him. He ducks.

'Christ!' he says.

She takes the frying pan off the hob and walks towards him.

'Be reasonable,' he says, just before she hurls the pan at him. She misses his head but some of the fried food strikes him.

'Fuck sake,' he says, shocked, as a piece of bacon slides off his shoulder to join the other half-cooked rashers and sausages that lie on the floor.

'Go, before I kill you.' She's grasping the wok now, with both hands, as if it were a tennis racquet. As he runs into the corridor, she flings the contents at his retreating back.

Esmé turns off the gas rings and the oven. Minutes later, she hears the front door slam. She surveys the desecration in her kitchen. The lamb's heart is the only piece of meat that's still complete and raw.

IS THIS LIKE SCOTLAND?

Fintan can smell warm chips as he enters the pub. His stomach rumbles, but it can't be heard above the low-volume anguish of 'Tainted Love' that emanates from a jukebox in the corner.

'I haven't heard that in years,' Fintan observes, as he leads his father-in-law, Sven, to a comfortable seat in the corner. 'When was it in the charts? Late eighties, maybe?'

Sven doesn't know. He could pass for a West Cork farmer, in his sensible anorak and Wellingtons, but, in fact, he's a small-town Swedish dentist.

'So, Sven,' says Fintan. 'What'll you have?'

Sven knows. 'Bimmish.'

Fintan goes to the bar and orders two pints of Beamish. One good thing about Sven is that he appreciates a nice pint of stout. One bad thing is that he never buys a round. Fintan's plan was to bring his wife Annika to Ireland to see the land he came from, but Annika insisted on bringing her parents too. They've all been here three days now and Fintan's paid for everything so far: the meals, the hotels, the petrol. Everything.

Fintan watches the first pint flowing into the glass, the deep, almost opaque black liquid swirling, the tan-coloured froth rising to the top, and his mood lightens slightly. He remembers visits to Creedons Hotel in Inchigeela with his dad when he was a young boy. His father would drink 'one for the road' and Fintan would have red lemonade and a packet of Taytos. Then they'd head home in the grey Morris Minor, up the mountain to Gortnahoughtee. The memory is so real Fintan jumps when the barmaid speaks to him.

'Would you like anything else?' she smiles.

'Could I have a packet of Taytos, please? Cheese and Onion, if you have them.'

Then Fintan turns his head towards Sven.

'Would you like some Taytos?' he asks. 'Or peanuts?'

'No.'

Fintan turns back to the barmaid and pays. A pint in each hand, he walks carefully over to Sven's table, places the pints reverently on beer mats. He goes back for the crisps, then settles into a chair next to Sven.

'There we go,' he says. 'Sláinte!'

Fintan and Sven clink their glasses together and then each takes a long slurp of beer.

Fintan begins to feel better, but he's still embittered about the fact that his in-laws don't offer to pay for anything. Not only that, he can't understand why they don't say 'Thank you'. Maybe it's a cultural thing, even a language thing, he muses. Maybe Swedish people don't say thanks unless it's a big deal. Come to think of it, 'Tak' is such a short, curt, *thankless* kind of word.

Fintan's been married for less than a year. He bought the house in North London three years ago, then his previous girlfriend said *You're a nice guy, Fintan, but I don't love you any more. The spark has gone.* A few months later his father, a widower, died. After the funeral Fintan lost interest in his London home, left it half-furnished, spent long hours at work and more time in the pub than was advisable.

Then the slim blonde Cindy-doll moved into a bed-sit in the house next to his and thrilled him back to his former self. Annika, for it was she, was forever knocking on his door for help: lost keys, a suspected rat, a leaky radiator, she'd run out of cigarettes... She thrilled him so much he overlooked the fact that she never said 'Thank you'... or even 'Tak'.

When her landlord threw her out, Annika moved in with him. The sex was amazing — after a week of cohabitation, he proposed to her. She said 'Yes', but didn't fancy the ring. They went to Aspreys in New Bond Street where she chose one five times more expensive. 'Darling, this is the one I want,' she said. Mesmerised with happiness, he produced his credit card and willingly signed a piece of paper handed to him on a silver salver by the shop assistant, who wore an expensive suit.

She didn't say 'Thanks' or even 'Tak'. She was busy admiring the ring.

Fintan gulps his pint, shoves a handful of crisps in his mouth. He swallows too quickly and begins to choke, so he drinks some more, then wipes his mouth.

'So, Sven. How's the pint?'

'Gud.'

'I wonder how long they'll be?'

Silence.

'Will I get a menu?'

Sven nods and looks at his glass.

'I will, so.' Fintan's stomach rumbles in anticipation as he approaches the bar counter. He picks up four greasy laminated menus and walks back to where Sven sits, immobile.

'Jesus, I'm hungry all the time,' he says to Sven. 'Maybe I've worms.'

Sven looks at him.

'Forget it,' says Fintan.

They drink in silence.

The door opens and Annika bustles in with her mother. Annika carries several plastic bags. So does Annika's mother.

'Got a few bargains,' says Annika, as she takes a pair of designer rubber boots out of a bag. They're pink with a flower print.

'Only €69,' she says, briskly.

Fintan suspects she's used their joint credit card again but he's afraid to ask. She gets cross when he tries to discuss money, though he's explained he wouldn't mind so much if she'd only warn him in advance of the financial shocks that seem to punctuate his existence these days.

Annika's mother wants mint tea.

'I think we have some out the back,' says the barmaid. She disappears.

'Lovely girl, that,' says Fintan.

Annika looks at him and raises her eyebrows.

Annika's mother looks round but it's hard to tell what her mood is. Her hands are bony and much older than her face, which seems taut and drawn, as if she's struggling against a high wind. Fintan's not supposed to know about her face-lift. Annika warned him not to mention it.

'Is this place okay?' asks Fintan.

'Yah,' says Annika's mother.

'So why the...' says Fintan. He nearly said *So why the long face?* Since they set off from London, the number of times he's almost mentioned cosmetic surgery is phenomenal.

'Where's that girl gone?' says Annika, crossly. 'She could have grown the tea by now.'

After lunch, they stroll down the street. The sun is shining and a salty breeze floats in from the bay. The rented Land Rover is parked near the edge of the water and looks as if it's in a television advert.

'Fabulous machine, isn't it?' says Fintan. He pats the dashboard fondly. 'I'd love one of these.'

'I thought you didn't approve of wrecking the environment,' says Annika as she settles herself in the front passenger seat.

'Well, if we lived here it would be practical,' says Fintan. 'Especially where we're going next.' As he pulls away from the kerb, he turns on the radio. *There's not enough love to go around, there's... not enough,* croons a male voice.

'Too loud!' shouts Annika's mother from the back seat.

'Yah, too loud,' Sven agrees.

'Okay, okay,' says Fintan.

Annika turns the radio down.

Sunlight streams into the car. Fintan fumbles around the dashboard, finds his sunglasses, puts them on.

'Do you like it here?' he asks his wife, as he drives. 'Isn't it better than North London?'

'It's different.'

'It sure is. Remember the gun battles in Green Lanes a few years back? In 2003? Sure, North London was like the Wild West.'

'Really?' Annika says, querulously.

'Do you not remember? My old pal Attila, who owns the greengrocers at the corner—he nearly got shot in the cross-fire.'

'Really?' says Annika.

'He kept that pumpkin for ages, the one with the bullet inside it. "Exhibit A", he called it. I walked past his shop a few minutes before the shoot-out. It could have been *my* head.'

'Well, I like London. You have a good job there. My pay is not so high as yours, but I get staff discount on my clothes...'

'So... you wouldn't consider moving here then?' He takes his eyes off the road to look at her.

'London is okay,' she says.

Fintan hasn't said anything to Annika about the field. It's a surprise.

When his mother died, he was only six years old; his memories of her have faded now, mixed up with images from old photographs. Fintan remembers everything about Dad though. It was just the two of them together for years, working the farm, and taking care of 'the field above'. His father had been sentimental about 'the field above'. He'd managed to hold onto it, even through bad times. *When I've money, Fintan*, he'd say, *I'll do up that house. For it's in that house, as you know, that I was born.*

Fintan has sold the farm but kept the field. The little house that sits inside it has been derelict for years. It's a house-type common round here; two-up, two-down, overgrown with ivy and creepers. An architect friend was enthusiastic: *It's a fantastic site, Fintan. I'd love to do a design for you. Modern extension to the back, lots of glass, double-height space... We'll keep the old house at the front — make sure we respect the vernacular. Lovely.*

'Where are we going?' says Annika. 'Is it to the Google Barry place you talked of?'

'No,' he says. 'We're going up the mountain. You'll love it. We can go to Gougane Barra tomorrow if you like.' His stomach rumbles.

As Fintan drives up the mountain, the road gets narrower and bumpier until it's no more than a boreen. Finally, he parks in front of an overgrown hedge, behind which the derelict cottage hides.

He opens the dilapidated farm gate at the side of the house and walks into the field. Sunlight hits broken glass on the path behind the house. It's so quiet that he can hear a rabbit before it scurries across the field a few feet in front of him just as Annika and her parents trail behind him.

'Is it muddy?' says Annika. 'I don't want to ruin my shoes.'

Fintan stares at the clouds that hang over the valley below. They seem so near the edge of the mountain; they look as if you could touch them. He remembers a time when he believed he could step on one of these clouds and float away. It's warm, even though there's a slight breeze. The Coillte forests that line the hills are felled in uneven patches and remind him of a bad haircut. Only one farmhouse can be seen, miles away. There are shades of greens and blues and greys and browns everywhere, and as the clouds change so do the shadows on the nearby hills.

Fintan knows that in winter time the wind blows wild up here and makes the old gate whistle a tune that no one else can sing. He knows that if he shouts, he'll hear his own voice echo back from the other hills and across the forest. He's always loved that echo and the illusion it creates that he is not alone.

But now, Sven ruins his view. He's walking along the perimeter of the field and he seems to be counting his steps.

Fintan decides to ignore him and glances in the other direction where his mother-in-law stands next to Annika. Maybe it's the facelift — no, it's not just that. Annika's profile is remarkably similar to that of her mother. Fintan can see the nose (a little too big), the determined chin, the slight — but ever-present — downturn of dissatisfaction on the edge of the mouth.

Annika's mother seems to like the view.

'So, what do you think?' asks Fintan. 'It's beautiful, isn't it?'

There's a pause.

'Is this like Scotland?' says Annika's mother.

Fintan takes a deep breath.

'Why did you bring us here?' says Annika. 'It's just a field.'

Fintan thinks for a moment.

'No reason,' he says. 'No reason at all.'

WAITING FOR THE BULLET

My husband Turlough arrived home with the gun a few weeks ago. I heard him coming in from work and putting his laptop on the hall table as usual, then the sound of packaging being ripped open as he strode into the kitchen. Turlough's an immediate presence, full of energy. When I first met him this thrilled me, but lately it makes me feel — not tired exactly — maybe just a little diminished.

'Look at this!' he said. 'It's brilliant.' He threw the gun onto the worktop. It was made of metal and the butt was beige-coloured plastic.

'Jesus!' I said.

'Ah, cop yourself on, Melissa. It's only a toy.' He picked it up, pressed something and the barrel fell open. 'Look, this is how you load it.'

He took a red plastic circle from a tube, pushed it into the exposed cylinder and clicked it shut. Then he pointed the gun at my face and pressed the trigger. The sharp crack of the gunshot sounded so real that I ducked. A haze of smoke hung in the air and behind it Turlough laughed. 'You should see your face! Isn't it convincing?'

'It's horrible,' I said.

'Ah, it's only a bit of fun.'

'Let's put it away,' I said. I shoved it into the junk drawer and began to make dinner.

The junk drawer is part of an ugly armoire that my mother-in-law gave us. 'It's an heirloom,' she said, but I suspect she was yearning to get rid of it. If I could, I'd junk the entire piece of furniture. There's one big drawer at the base, and that's where I put stuff destined for the charity shop or the dustbin — things I can't throw away immediately, usually because they belong to Turlough.

That night, while Turlough was out playing tennis, I contemplated the contents of the junk drawer. The first thing I saw was a cigarette lighter shaped like a woman with 'Souvenir of Lanzarote' engraved on it — it was about time I got rid of that. Among various other useless objects, there was a Casio pocket viewer (unused since he got his Blackberry) and a candy-striped tie from Brown Thomas that made him look like a pimp... The gun was there too, nestling between a packet of condoms in the colours of the Irish flag and a key-ring with a plastic pint of Guinness attached. I took the gun out and became oddly fascinated by it. I loaded it, aimed at the fridge and shut my eyes, then pressed the trigger. The sound was loud and convincing.

I fired six more times, aiming through the window at birds and a stray cat, until I hardly jumped at the noise any more. Finally, I looked in the mirror and shot myself in the head. As I put the gun away, I felt strangely fulfilled.

I was reading in bed when Turlough lurched in.

'Night,' he said as he lowered himself into bed and turned on his side. I moved close to him but he didn't turn around, just said, 'You haven't forgotten that Stacey and Richard are coming over tomorrow night?'

'No, I haven't,' I said. 'Why?'

'Just wondering. You know she doesn't like goat's cheese, don't you?'

'Yes. Do you want me to recite the menu?'

'No, I'm sure it'll be fine.' He kissed me perfunctorily and was snoring within minutes. I lay awake next to him and tried not to think about the fact that we hadn't had sex in months. Then I went to the bathroom and lay on the bathmat for a while with a hand towel and fingers between my thighs. As I flushed the toilet later, I told myself that relationships were like economies, that they were cyclical things, with peaks and troughs. That me and Turlough were just temporarily in recession.

The dinner party was partly business and partly pleasure. 'Greasing the Wheels of Industry,' Turlough calls it. I feel like a fraud when I have to be nice to his clients, but he says it's essential. Everyone in Ireland seems to smell recession in the air, and Turlough's a building contractor so he needs to keep on top of things. I'm an editorial assistant at *Free Ads Weekly* — we'd never survive on my income alone.

Turlough seemed nervous that night. He looked fit, though, in his casual striped shirt and chinos — younger than his forty years.

'Have you chilled the champagne?' he asked.

'Yes,' I said, as I fastened my necklace. 'Everything's under control.'

The doorbell rang and I dabbed at my lipstick while he ran downstairs.

I heard Stacey's loud voice.

'It's fantastic to see you again, Turlough!' she said.

As I came downstairs, she was holding both of his hands, telling him how handsome he looked.

'There you are!' she exclaimed, when she saw me. 'Long time, no see!'

She kissed me once on each cheek and her perfume, like her voice, overwhelmed me. I wondered if she'd been drinking. She was dressed expensively in black and seemed flushed, excited. I felt dowdy — I'd forgotten to take my apron off.

'Where's Richard?' I asked.

'Paying the taxi,' she replied. 'Oh, here he is!'

Richard came in, shook Turlough's hand and kissed my cheek, saying, 'Lovely to see you, Melissa.'

I took the coats while Turlough led the way.

'How about a champagne cocktail?' Turlough was already swinging into his 'life and soul of the party' mode.

'Sounds fabulous, darling,' said Stacey.

'I wouldn't say no,' said Richard, spearing an olive.

At first, the evening went well. The cocktails set the pace, and I prepared an entrée of king prawns with garlic and coriander in a creamy tomato sauce while the others kept drinking. As I cleared the starters I noticed the first bottle of white wine was empty, so I brought another into the dining room and handed the corkscrew to Turlough. As I did, he gave me one of those grateful glances he'd not given me for a long time, and I smiled back, before going off to check the meat. As I warmed the milk for the mash and then pummelled it, the asparagus steaming and the lamb resting, I felt more confident than I'd been in ages. Then I remembered the red wine specially chosen by Turlough. I trotted to the dining room and gave it to him. All three were chatting busily. I went back to the kitchen.

The food smelled good. I plated it like they do on *MasterChef*, a sprig of fresh rosemary on top of each pyramid of lamb, a curve of mash, a fan of green and gold vegetables, a smooth brown lake of gravy. I went back to the dining room with a plate in each hand and moved round the table to serve Stacey from her right. As she leaned towards Turlough, I had a sudden memory of working in a place called Chez Jacques twenty years previously and for a moment it felt as if they were on a date and I was their waitress.

We took a break after the main course. I cleared the plates and returned to the table with the coffee pot.

Turlough sluiced cognac into brandy glasses, then sat down heavily. 'We brought this back from our last trip to France,' he said. I poured coffee and splashed a little on the tablecloth.

'Oops, poor Melissa is a bit tipsy,' Stacey said, wagging her finger at me and nudging Turlough in the ribs.

'I'm not,' I said. 'I'm just a bit tired.'

'No wonder,' said Richard and turned to me. 'Have you been following the U.S. election at all? What do you think of McCain's running mate, that Sarah Palin?'

'I think she's dreadful,' I said.

'But she's a strong woman,' said Stacey. 'I admire strong women.'

'She's frightening, she's…' I stopped.

'She's gutsy!' exclaimed Stacey. 'I don't agree with all of her policies, of course, but she's no pushover.'

'Well, she can shoot a gun anyway,' observed Richard.

Turlough began to laugh. 'Anyone can shoot a gun,' he said. 'I'll show you. Where's my weapon, Melissa?'

'I'll get it,' I said. I left the room and came back with the gun.

'This thing is hilarious,' Turlough told them. He pushed the trigger but nothing happened.

'It needs reloading,' I said. I took out the used ring cap, replaced it with a fresh one and handed it back. Turlough aimed at the wine bottle and shot it several times. Stacey and Richard jumped in alarm, then howled with laughter.

'I want a go!' exclaimed Stacey.

'We'll all have a turn,' said Turlough and handed it to her.

Stacey shot her husband several times and he died a mock death, writhing next to me in his chair, his head in a gunpowder halo. Then Richard took the gun. He shot Stacey once, then pulled the trigger again. This time, there was no sound, just a click as the trigger fell back.

'Needs more ammo,' said Turlough.

Richard turned to me, still holding the weapon. 'Don't you want to have a go?' he asked.

'Yes,' I said. 'I have a great idea.'

I took the gun from him and used the corkscrew to dig out seven of the eight little shots from a new ring cap. Then I fitted it into the gun barrel and pressed the trigger eight times. Only one shot rang out.

'That's it,' I said. I repeated the procedure with another ring cap and pushed it into place. 'The four of us can play Russian Roulette. Just like the film.' I gave the cylinder a quick spin and clicked the gun shut.

'What film?' Stacey asked.

'*The Deer Hunter.*'

'Oh. I didn't see that.'

'Yes, you did,' said Richard. 'Robert de Niro was in it.'

'It doesn't matter,' I said. 'You'll see as we go along.'

Turlough seemed apprehensive.

'Brilliant!' said Richard. 'I'll go first.'

Bravely, he put the gun barrel to his temple. Turlough kept quiet. Stacey began to laugh.

'Stop,' said Richard. 'Don't make me laugh, you'll ruin the effect. Gosh, this feels surprisingly scary.' He pulled the trigger and nothing was heard except a click.

'Me next,' I said. I grabbed the gun, placed it to my temple as he had, and pulled the trigger. Click.

Turlough grabbed the gun dramatically and waved it like a matinee idol in an old black and white film, then shot himself in the forehead. The explosion sounded real. Everyone jumped.

'Christ,' he said. 'It *is* loud, isn't it?'

'I've not had my go,' said Stacey.

'Well,' I said. 'You're alive, aren't you? That's the whole point.' I took out the spent ring cap and prepared another round, again leaving only one live shot in place. 'Who's first this time?'

'Me,' said Richard. 'Let's go round in a clockwise direction.'

'Okay. Don't forget to give it a bit of a spin.'

Richard fired a blank.

Stacey fired a blank.

Turlough hesitated before he fired. A shot rang out.

'You're dead,' I said.

'Not again...' he moaned.

I readied the gun again and fired a blank.

Next, Richard fired a blank.

Stacey waited and winced.

'Go on,' I said.

'Hurry up,' said Richard.

Turlough just waited, staring wide-eyed at her.

She fired. It was a blank.

Turlough fired and the shot seemed louder than before.

'I'm dead again,' he screeched. 'This is freaking me out.'

'Let's do it again,' I said.

'It's a one-in-eight chance if there are eight shots in each round, so what's the odds...?' Richard calculated in his head.

'Who wants to start?' I asked.

'Me,' said Turlough. 'I want to get it over with.' He pointed the gun at his temple this time, made a funny face, pulled the trigger. He gasped when the shot rang out. 'Fucking weird,' he said. 'We should stop this.'

'No,' said Richard. 'It's fun. Anyway, *you* can't die again, Turlough, can you? It's just not mathematically possible.'

'One more,' I said. 'There's one set of bullets left.'

'Let's go anti-clockwise this time. Me first,' said Richard. He tried several facial expressions. 'I'm imagining myself in the film,' he said. 'I'm Christopher Walken...' He contorted his face in simulated agony.

'Get a move on,' said Stacey.

'Shut up,' he said. He took a deep breath, pulled the trigger. It clicked impotently.

Before anyone could move, I took the gun, put the gun barrel in my mouth and fired. Click.

I passed it to Turlough. He fired at his forehead, a strange look on his face. Click. 'I don't believe it. I'm alive.'

Stacey was next. 'I don't think I like this game any more,' she said. She shut her eyes and squeezed the trigger. The shot was so loud I expected blood, and the bullet left a smoky aura round her head. She sat there, holding the gun, not saying a word.

'You're dead, Stacey,' said Richard. 'And it's time to go home.'

I stood at the door and waved goodbye as the rear lights of the taxi vanished into the night.

'Well, that's the last we'll see of her,' I said. 'She's history.'

'What do you mean?' said Turlough.

'You know what I mean.'

'For Christ' sake,' he said. 'I don't know what you're getting at.'

I felt beaten.

'And anyway...' he added.

'I know what you're going to say. I forgot the dessert.'

'To hell with the dessert.' He swallowed the last of his brandy and put the glass down. Then he came towards me and began to grope me like he hadn't done in years. We didn't even reach our bed — half-torn clothes on the carpet, sucking and fucking like mad things.

He didn't roll away afterwards. He just lay there on top of me. Only his chest heaved, as he cried quietly. I lay underneath him, my arms outstretched. I couldn't seem to raise them, not even to comfort him.

I've taken the gun out of the junk drawer and looked at it several times since then. I know I should throw it out, but I can't seem to let it go.

THE WOLF NOTE

Eddie is sitting at his desk shooting pheasants on his new iPhone. He lines up each virtual pheasant in the crosshairs on the screen and every time he shoots one, the phone reverberates satisfyingly. He's almost surpassed his personal best when the phone rings and he loses concentration. It rings again. He sighs and answers the call.

'What is it, Eileen? I'm a bit busy this morning.'

'The Santa has let us down,' says his wife. 'You'll have to do it.'

'No way.'

'We're really stuck. Come on. You never do anything for the kids.'

'Look, I *do* do things, I'm *trying...*'

'Oh, you're trying all right,' she says. 'You're *very* trying.' This is something she used to say as a joke, but it's no longer funny. 'Look, the PTA has put a lot of work into the kids' party and we've got to have a Santa. You're it.'

'Who says *I'm* it?'

'I do. You're not that busy. Get the costume from Rita and give yourself a couple of hours off—it's your own company, after all.'

Eddie hurries from his office through the cold air of the street and by the time he enters Brown Thomas on Patrick Street he's sweating. Inside the store, coloured spotlights illuminate the faces of dazed shoppers and fake-tanned sales staff, while piped musak plays 'The Little Drummer Boy'... *parumpapumpum*....

He finds Rita, the yummy mummy, at the beauty counter on the ground floor. Rita is luscious-lipped and gorgeous but since her husband's Toyota dealership went bankrupt, there's an edge to her, an unhappiness that makes her even more desirable. Eddie wonders when the constant lust in his head began.

'I'm here for the costume,' he says.

'Great.' Rita smiles tensely. 'Can you cover for a few minutes?' she asks her colleague. Then she grabs a plastic bag and says to Eddie, 'Follow me.'

Eddie admires her bum as he follows her up two flights of escalators. In the Men's Department she hands him the bag.

'The changing rooms are over there,' she says.

Eddie goes into a changing room and takes off his coat. His small paunch depresses him, but at least his skin rash has cleared up. The Udo's Oil that Eileen made him take for months has worked, and even the skin on his elbows is silky smooth.

He puts the Santa suit on over his clothes, then the hat and a pair of round Santa glasses. He looks at himself in the full-length mirror and feels like killing Eileen. The Santa outfit is meant for a bigger man. It sags everywhere, even when he puts on the black plastic belt, and he has to roll up the trouser legs. His brown shoes don't go with the rest of the outfit. The beard is itchy and uncomfortable, so he pushes it down until it hangs round his neck like an odd fluffy necktie. Morosely, he leaves the changing room and trudges toward the escalator, carrying his coat in the plastic bag.

As Eddie descends the escalator dressed as Santa, he's devastated to see smart-ass bachelor-about-town Garvan Grady coming up the adjacent elevator towards him. Garvin is forty and footloose. He goes to the gym and the swimming pool and the tanning shop and on holidays where he has one-night stands with girls who wear bikinis and sarongs during the day and absolutely nothing at night and give oral sex and every other kind of sex imaginable and never want commitment. Apparently he's been dating a nineteen-year-old recently. Garvan wouldn't be seen dead in a stupid Santa outfit.

Eddie looks in the opposite direction as the escalator he stands on moves slowly downwards. Garvan continues to ascend. He's wearing a brown suede jacket with a striped scarf around his neck. Eddie draws in his stomach, grabs his dangling Santa beard and hurriedly pushes it up onto his face. *Act normal,* he tells himself. *Act like a regular Santa.* He can't resist a sideways glance at Garvan as he passes, and seconds later his cover is blown.

'Eddie! It's you, Eddie! You madman — what's with the Santa Claus gear?' Garvan's looking back, he's almost at the top of the escalator, now he's there, he's turned round at the top, he's bounding down *Eddie's* escalator and within seconds he's standing next to Eddie on the ground floor.

'Ah Garvan… I didn't see you there.'

'You're up to no good, I betcha.'

'I wish,' says Eddie. 'No, I'm doing a kids' party over at the school.'

'No way,' marvels Garvan. 'I thought you were going to an office party. Not that you need a disguise to get you in the festive mood, ha?' He nudges Eddie playfully.

'Well…,' says Eddie.

'Are you going to the gig tonight?'

'What gig?'

'Did you not get the e-mail?' says Garvan. 'All the lads will be there.'

'I didn't. Look, I have to go. I'll be late.'

'Boys' night out. You must come.'

'I can't,' says Eddie. 'Eileen has her book club tonight.'

'Come on. I've a spare ticket. Meet me for a drink at five, we'll head into the show at seven.'

Fuck it, thinks Eddie. *It's the least I deserve.* 'Okay. I'll be there.'

Rain drizzles weakly as Eddie walks out of the school gates. *Never again,* he thinks to himself. *Not in a million years.*

The children had been noisy and rude. One Junior Infant had cried when he said, 'Ho ho ho and a Merry Christmas'. Two others had yanked his beard. His younger son, in Senior Infants, had merely looked confused. His daughter took no notice of Santa at all. She was busy chatting to her friend — after all, she was ten and had probably met at least a dozen Santas by now. His older son Fergus had stated loudly (in a manner that reminded Eddie of his wife), that he wanted a Wii for Christmas. Eddie had had the presence of mind to say, 'Ho, ho, ho, very funny,' only to hear Fergus say, even louder, 'It's not Santa, it's my dad,' while a teacher said, 'Shush' weakly. What kind of teachers were they these days? Fuck-all discipline. All the children were spoilt rotten and the carol-singing they did for Santa was, frankly, diabolical.

Eddie trudges back to the department store to divest himself of his costume.

'How was it?' Rita asks.

'Dire.' He's not in the mood for small talk and he's starving. He decides to go for a late lunch.

Eddie sits by himself in the Farmgate restaurant in front of a generous bowl of Irish stew. It's so good he orders apple tart with custard and a cup of coffee. This is the kind of life he deserves. In a fit of bravado he takes out his phone and texts his wife.

> Dear Eileen Santa mission accomplished.
> Did u know Fergus wants Wii for xmas?

> Going out to gig with lads tonite, see u
> wen I see u. Cheers, Eddie.

As he takes another bite of apple tart, the phone buzzes.

> Out of the question. My book club tonite.
> I need u home 6pm sharp. What do u mean
> Fergus wants a Wii?

He sighs, imagines Eileen's fury if he doesn't do the necessary. He thinks about nights out with the lads when he was young, before the kids, back when Eileen was still nice to him. He remembers his earlier humiliation, drinks the last of his coffee. *It's pathetic. I can't even suggest a night out with the lads without getting a bollicking,* he fumes, while he waits to pay his bill.

'Fuck it,' he says, out loud. He hands the alarmed waiter a twenty, says, 'Keep the change' and leaves. Outside, he taps another text to his wife.

> No can do.

He presses 'Send' quickly. His phone buzzes angrily a few seconds later.

> What do u mean NO CAN DO?

He texts again.

> I'm out 2night with the lads. Forgot to
> mention it. Sorry. See u tomorrow.

The phone buzzes again. He turns it off.

Eddie feels like an outlaw. As far as he's concerned, he's now gone over to the dark side. In an incredibly short space of time he purchases a new shirt, jeans and a fine dark green suede jacket in a shop on Oliver Plunkett Street. Then he buys a travel kit from Boots, which contains a mini-shaving kit, a mini-toothbrush and toothpaste, plus various other mini-necessities. He takes an old rug from the boot of his car, goes back to his office, unplugs his desk phone, turns off his iPhone and sleeps for two hours on the floor. When he wakes, he uses everything in his travel kit and hums 'Have Yourself a Merry Little Christmas' while he shaves and dresses.

On his way out, the receptionist calls from the glass-bound desk in the foyer.

'Your wife called the main desk, Eddie.'

'Tell her I'm gone,' says Eddie.

Garvan's already sitting at the bar when Eddie strides in at 5 p.m.

'Fair play, you made it!' says Garvan.

'What's the show, anyway? Where's the lads?'

'Well,' says Garvan. 'I'm not entirely sure who's coming. Jim can't make it because his wife's away. Martin has a client meeting at six so he'll meet us later. Frank's coming, I *think*, and maybe Richie. Ben will definitely be here.'

After three pints Eddie's astounded that he ever considered Garvan a pain in the neck. As the pub gets busy, Garvan tries to chat up a woman sitting on the next bar stool, but she's more interested in talking to Eddie.

'Did anyone text you?' says Garvan, disgruntled, when the woman leaves them to join her friends.

'I don't know. I turned my phone off.'

Ben arrives, out of breath. 'I made it,' he says. 'I thought I'd never get away.'

Eddie buys the next round and goes to the Gents. In the toilet he turns on his phone and finds there are two messages. The first is long and indignant:

> You selfish prick nothing was discussed about u going out tonight. wat kind of way is this to behave?

The second is sorrowful.

> U don't even want to speak to me. It's very hurtful. I no things not perfect but u cud at least reply to my text.

Shamed, he texts back:

> Sorry missed texts. Had to turn phone off during show. Will make it up to you. Speak later.

He returns to the bar and shows Ben and Garvan his new phone. 'I'm going to get one of those,' says Garvan, enviously.

Eddie finds out, to his delight, how to change the ring tone to a cheerful snippet of 'Blame it on the Boogie'. He plays it until Ben says, 'Turn it off. You're annoying people,' so he does.

Eddie, Garvan and Ben settle into their numbered seats.

'What's the name of the band?' asks Eddie.

'Shh,' says Garvan as a group of people in semi-formal clothes walk onto a stage filled with keyboards and brass instruments and guitars and music stands.

'Is this jazz?' hisses Eddie. 'I thought it was a normal gig.'

A dapper man with a goatee beard wearing a suit and two-tone shoes walks to the front of the stage and says, 'Now, we begin.'

Eddie sits back and watches. The cellist is wearing a black dress and high-heeled leopard-skin shoes and Eddie can't concentrate on the music—he's too busy imagining her in leopard-skin underwear and black-lace stockings and suspenders, with her legs wrapped around the cello, while she plays it just for him.

At the end of the show Garvan chats to the cellist. When he returns he announces, 'Okay lads, we're meeting the band in the pub.'

In the Corner House pub, Garvan confides, 'That doll on the cello? I've met her before and tonight is her lucky night. I happen to know she's gagging for it.'

'Oh Jesus,' says Ben. 'Not again. Do you know what we call him, Eddie? "The Fog".'

'Why?'

'You know the way one minute the sky is clear and next thing, before you know it, the fog is on top of you? Garvan's like that with women.'

'So how are you going to chat her up?'

'I've done research,' says Garvan, confidently. 'On the Wolf Note.'

'The Wolf Note?' says Eddie. 'What's that?'

'Ah, this'll get her going all right. Listen.'

Garvan explains that most cellos have a problem note called the Wolf Note — one pitch that sounds annoyingly different from all the others. Depending on the instrument, it can even have audible beats to it, and sound rather like a sick cow. It's a result of the instability between the vibration of the body of the cello and the vibration of the affected string, which then cancel each other out. The cello has to be adjusted, he says; the sound post at that point must be tightened or made longer. Unfortunately, there is no permanent solution; it's a case of constant adjustment.

Garvan sounds like he's learnt this off by heart. Strangely enough, he says the better the instrument, the worse the Wolf Note can be.

'You want to maximise the sound of the instrument, apparently,' he adds. 'But minimise the Wolf.'

The band arrive in the pub. Eddie finds himself sitting beside the delectable cellist and he begins to talk about the Wolf Note. 'I wonder if I'm right in thinking...' he says. He astounds himself by how knowledgeable he sounds. The cellist, whose name is Clodagh, is happy to discuss the Wolf Note, and they give the matter a thorough airing. Eddie notices Garvan glaring but he ignores him. He buys more drink for himself and the cellist and at some stage in the proceedings he finds himself outside the pub, pressing Clodagh against the back wall, his mouth glued to hers as if he were having his first ever 'shift', age nineteen, outside Spyder's Nite Club.

'Let's go home,' she says.

Eddie feels a bit unsteady on his feet so he holds Clodagh's hand tightly as she leads him towards Wellington Road.

'Here we are,' she says, stopping before a tall building. She has trouble handling her keys but eventually she succeeds in opening the heavy front door. Eddie follows her up two flights of stairs and waits, slightly out of breath, while she unlocks the door of her apartment.

'Gotta go to the jacks,' she giggles and leaves Eddie standing in a room that seems to be a sitting room, kitchen and diner all at once. The table is cluttered with plates and glasses. Saucepans sit in the sink.

He hears the toilet flush, then Clodagh returns.

'Come on, big boy,' she says and brings him into the bedroom. Collages of clothes are strewn across the bed. She sweeps them onto the floor, then turns off the light and throws herself into bed.

In the dark, Eddie takes off his new green suede jacket and his shoes, and joins her. She's naked already so he takes off the rest of his clothes under the quilt until he's just wearing his underpants. They roll around in the bed and kiss until she's moaning loudly and he's rearing to go.

'Have you got a condom?' she whispers.

'Eh, no,' says Eddie.

'Shit.' She switches on the bedside light and rolls onto her stomach. As she fumbles in the drawer of the bedside cabinet, Eddie notices the dimpled skin on the back of her thighs and feels himself wilt.

'I've run out,' she says. 'Shit. Party's over. You're probably fucking married anyway.'

'Eh, yeah,' says Eddie apologetically, glancing at his wedding ring. Clodagh begins to cry.

'Ah now,' says Eddie. 'Now, now, now.' He looks at her for a moment, then gathers her up and strokes her drunkenly while she weeps. Soon, his hand is on her vulva, pressing it rhythmically as she moves against it. Expertly, he kneads her with his fingers until she comes. Shortly afterwards, she falls asleep.

Eddie rises from the bed and gathers his clothing furtively. Clodagh mumbles something unintelligible in her sleep and he stands still for a moment and stares at her. There's something about the way she's curled up in the quilt... a memory rises in his sore head, a long-ago image of his wife Eileen, at home in exhausted slumber, only a day or so after the birth of their first-born son. He remembers watching over mother and child in prideful fear, picking the baby up when he cried, the first confusing nappy-change, the smell of the greenish-black meconium in the tiny diaper—he remembers wondering how something that was shit could smell so sweet.

Bundling his clothing under one arm and holding his shoes in the other hand, he leaves the bedroom stealthily. In the bathroom he dresses hastily, then urinates, washes his hands and splashes water on his face. There's a tube of toothpaste on a grimy glass shelf near the sink so he puts some on an index finger and rubs it around his gums, then spits it out forcefully, splattering saliva and toothpaste all over the bathroom mirror. He grabs some toilet paper and tries to wipe the mirror clean, but it's already smudged with some kind of make-up cream, or maybe it's mouthwash, and the toilet paper only makes it worse. *What on earth am I doing?* he wonders. *I never do this at home.* He wipes the surface frantically with a grimy face towel but the mirror's a streaky mess so he gives up and leaves.

Downstairs, as Eddie pulls the heavy front door closed behind him, the cold air of the street shocks him into near-sobriety. Standing under a weak yellow streetlight, he checks the time on his watch. It's

6 a.m. He shivers while he searches in the pockets of his costly suede jacket. Eventually, he locates his phone and switches it on.

There are no new messages.

AN UNDER-RATED EMOTION

I wake up in a strange room.

'We didn't use a condom last night,' Deirdre says. She's lying next to me in the bed. 'Are you worried?'

'What?'

'I was just wondering.'

My head is throbbing from last night's drinking and it's only just dawned on me that we're in New York, not Cork, and that I'm in a hotel bedroom. I can hardly bear to open my eyes. I turn my head towards Deirdre and I can smell that expensive body lotion she uses. She's on her back, looking up at the ceiling. Everything's too bright. I close my eyes again.

'Oh God,' I groan. 'I'm in agony. Did you bring any paracetamol with you?'

'Yeah,' she says. 'I'll get you some, birthday boy.' She leans over to kiss me.

'I wouldn't come too close if I were you,' I say. 'I bet my breath smells foul.'

'Well,' she says. 'You're probably right. You drank a fair bit last night. You had two pints at Shannon Airport and two double gins on the plane before it was even officially your birthday.'

'It was the beginning of my special birthday outing though,' I say, defensively. I wish I'd remembered to close the curtains.

'Yes, you explained that to everyone on the plane. You told the flight attendant she was gorgeous. You said she was your favourite air hostess ever, several times. I tried to stop you but you kept on saying it. *Air hostess*. I'd say they haven't been called that since the 1950s.'

'Ah, I was only joking.' I try to laugh it off. I'm a lot older than Deirdre. She's twenty-nine. I'm forty-six. No wonder she thinks I'm a dinosaur sometimes.

'Do you remember anything else?' she asks.

'Well, we checked into the hotel, didn't we? Then we had a bite to eat somewhere. I think we had a few drinks in the hotel bar after that.'

'You told everyone there it was your birthday too.'

'Then I suppose... em...'

'We came up here,' she says. 'Then you started the naked dancing. You wanted me to admire you in your birthday suit. That's when you made a lunge at me.'

'Oh Jesus, I remember now.' I feel the bedspread. 'God, the cover on this bed is so slippery. I'd have been alright only for that.'

Deirdre is laughing now. 'You were way off-course.'

'Jesus, it's all coming back to me. I slid straight across the bed and ended up on the floor—hit my head an awful whack against the skirting board.'

'I thought you'd knocked yourself out.'

'Oh God, I threw up, didn't I?' I shift sideways to the edge of the bed and look down, hoping there's no evidence on the carpet.

'Only in the bathroom,' Deirdre says.

'Thank fuck for that. Will you get me some painkillers?'

'Yeah.' She gets out of bed and puts on a silky floral dressing gown I don't remember seeing before. 'Anyway, you were fine a few hours later. You got very lively then. That's when we didn't use a condom, and you said… you don't remember what you said, do you?'

Deirdre orders breakfast from room service but all I can manage is coffee and a slice of toast and even that makes me feel queasy. I go back to bed and bunch the slippery quilt around me. The television's on low volume and the CNN weather girl says it might snow.

'We're in New York, for God's sake,' says Deirdre. 'Let's do something.'

'Sight-seeing isn't really my thing.'

'Let's go and see the Brooklyn Bridge,' she insists.

I don't tell her I've already been there, years ago, when I was promoting my first novel. I'm in no condition to argue.

'So long as we get taxis,' I tell her. 'I'm too weak to deal with the subway.'

We leave the hotel lobby and walk down 56th Street in search of a cab. It's March and atrociously cold. I'm shivering in my parka, thinking maybe I should go to Macy's first to buy gloves and a warm sweater. Deirdre doesn't seem to feel the cold. She looks fantastic in a black coat, slim-line blue jeans and her new Italian boots. Her coat is unbuttoned and it swings around her body in the wind when we turn a corner. I can see that nice red sweater of hers underneath the coat. She's wearing her multi-coloured scarf as well, and a daft woolly cap.

'You look nice in your mad hat,' I tell her.

'I love this place,' she says, dancing along beside me. 'I feel like I'm in *Sex and the City* or *Friends* — one of those really American sitcoms.'

She smiles in my direction, that certain smile that shows off her even white teeth. It's a clever, self-deprecating smile, as if she's conscious of the potential for ridicule there is in every situation. It's a brave smile too. Deirdre is a one-off. I pretend in my head I've never seen her before so I can see her like other people on the street do; I realise she *could* be a star in a sitcom of her own. I start humming and slowly realise it's the cheesy *Mary Tyler Moore* theme song.

'You remind me of Mary Tyler Moore,' I say. 'It must be the cap.'

'What?'

'Oh, nothing.' It must be more than thirty years since the *Mary Tyler Moore Show* was on RTE; she won't have a clue what I'm talking about.

Not that she's stupid. Deirdre's normally fairly clued in. There are gaps though, notably the fact that she doesn't seem to realise I'm a has-been. Sure, I was fashionable once, but now the literary pages use words like 'venal' and 'unreconstructed'; I've no idea how to reconstruct myself and I'm not sure I'm able. A film was made of one of my short stories in 2008 and I was commissioned to write a play in 2009 so there was a bit of renewed interest in my work for a while, but it wore off quickly. My last novel didn't find a publisher and I hardly earned anything last year except the Cnuas from Aosdána.

As I'm thinking all this, I lag behind. Deirdre turns round and smiles. I glimpse the red sweater beneath her coat again, and now all I can think of is an old childhood rhyme:

> *A cold wind doth blow and we shall have snow*
> *and what will the robin do then, poor thing?*
> *She'll sit in the barn and keep herself warm*
> *and hide her head under her wing.*

I wonder why Deirdre bothers with me. Some young women are a bit daft. They think older men have 'more depth', that they're mature and appreciative, that older men have experience and expertise that will rub off on them. Sometimes, too, they think older fellas have money. Deirdre's different. In fact, she earns much more than me; she's even paying for this trip. She's smart as well as sexy. She laughs. She's independent. She's beautiful. She puts up with me. We've been going out for nearly a year now. It might even last.

Fuck it, who am I fooling? She'll find a decent bloke her own age, eventually. She'll want a nice house with en-suite bathrooms and leather settees, a two-car garage, babies. Especially babies. Babies with Deirdre's smile, Deirdre's hair, Deirdre's fine bones. If I could think of some way to make money I could give her most of that, but I'll never be able to give her the babies. I got a vasectomy years ago. That's when I was swanning around the literary scene in London with the lovely Sylvia, beautiful Sylvia, who couldn't possibly get pregnant, she said, because it would ruin her career as a catwalk model. *Grand,* I said. *No bother. I'll get the snip.* I hear she's living in Wiltshire now, with four kids, a husband and horses.

In the 'fall-out' time after Sylvia, I didn't bother using condoms for a while, until an odious literary groupie claimed she was carrying my baby. Of course I knew it was impossible but I didn't tell her why— just took the blood test and learnt my lesson. STDs are no fun either; no more riding bareback for me, thanks very much. I'm surprised I let my guard down last night.

And what did I say to Deirdre? It'll come back to me.

I'm lagging behind again.

'Wait,' I say to Deirdre and I flag down a yellow cab.

The driver is a big swarthy man about my age, with curly black hair balding on top and a tan leather jacket. It's immediately clear that he's the talkative kind, because he slides back the perspex window and leaves the partition open. Then he leans back, tilting his head a little to the right, so he can talk to us while he drives.

'You folks having fun in the Big Apple?' is his opening gambit. His driving style reminds me of movie car chases.

'Yes,' says Deirdre. She smiles and leans forward a little. 'We arrived last night. It's his birthday treat.'

'Gee, many happy returns, Mister. Oh boy, excuse me now, I gotta put on the news. You mind? I got my son over in Afghanistan — been some action going on over there I got to catch up on.'

The car radio crackles on. He adjusts a dial and I expect him to run a light or rear-end the car in front any second. My head is pounding again. I hope Deirdre remembered to bring the paracetamol. The reporter's voice sounds tinny and unreal:

Firefight in eastern Afghanistan… a Chinook helicopter was shot down by insurgents… Thirty Americans were killed, including twenty-two Navy SEALS… members of Team Six, a special operations unit… on its way to aid troops on the ground…

'You wanna bet?' the taxi driver says. He waves one hand in the air. 'My ex-wife Ida, she'll ring me right this second. She'll be yak-yak-yakkin' at me now. She don't know where her mind's gone, now our Benny's over there.'

'Well, I'm not surprised,' says Deirdre. 'If I had …'

A terrible small noise fills the cab. It's a particularly virulent ring tone.

'Hey, Ida, how ya doin'?' the driver yells into his car phone. 'Whass'up?' He looks back and winks at me, and raises his eyes to heaven.

'*I'm worried about Benny,*' her voice replies faintly. '*Did you listen to the news just now?*'

'Why the hell you worried, Ida?'

'*I don't know,*' the woman says. '*I have a bad feeling.*'

'You're really something, you and your feelings,' the driver says, turning his head to wink at me again. 'I was just saying to folks I got in the cab here, you never quit worrying.'

'*But it's Benny out there, of course I'm worried. You aren't worried?*'

'No,' the driver says, laughing. 'And you know why? Because I listen to what they actually say on the radio. You, you never listen. Always a problem with you, Ida. Why don't you listen? Maybe you'd talk more sense if you listened.'

'*I listen, Henry, sure I listen, but…*'

'Listen to me good, Ida. Quit yakking and listen. What it is, is the ones in the helicopters were Navy SEALS, and our Benny isn't Navy, he's a paratrooper, Benny is, so what's to worry?'

'They said *thirty* casualties,' Deirdre mumbles. 'Only *twenty-two* of them were Navy.'

'*But Henry... there's this hotline for parents. Will you call them? Just call them. Please. For me.*' I think I can hear muffled sobs.

'Didn't I just tell you?' the driver insists. 'They said Navy SEALS. I'm not gonna call now like some kind of schmuck.'

All I can hear from the speaker of the car phone now is a kind of shuffling noise.

'You wanna act like a dumb ass?' he adds. 'So *you* call.'

'*Okay,*' she says, trying to sound tough. '*I'll call.*'

'Yeah, you call!' the driver says and hangs up. 'Don't listen to no one, my ex don't.'

I feel Deirdre tensing up next to me. She leans forward towards the open part of the perspex partition.

'What the hell are you on about?' she says, angrily. 'You stupid, stupid man. Can't you see she's got every right to be concerned? It's her son, for fuck's sake. If I had a son, I'd never *ever* let him go to war...'

She takes a breath and I think she's done. Instead, she starts up again and this time her voice is louder and she's practically shouting. '*You're* the dumb ass. *You* are. They said *thirty* casualties, and only *twenty-two* were Navy whatsits. She's his mother, why wouldn't she be scared?'

'Hey now, lady...'

'Jesus, Deirdre, lighten up, would you?'

She tells me to fuck off. Then she starts crying. We're near Brooklyn Bridge so I ask the cabbie to drop us off. I tip him too much and he gestures with his hands and looks at me in silent sympathy as Deirdre exits the cab.

When I get out Deirdre has already paced ahead. I catch up with her and grip her arm. As we walk onto the bridge, she shrugs her arm away and won't look at me. It's bitter cold up here as we walk along the boardwalk. The arcs of metal stretching upwards on either side are no protection from the wind. Tall buildings all around us shimmer in the water and shine in the cold grey sky.

'It's freezing. Button up your coat,' I say to Deirdre, as if she's a child, and she does. The breeze becomes stronger and sharp hailstones begin to pelt down.

Deirdre turns to me. Her face is blotchy.

'It's all right for him,' she shouts. 'He *has* a child. I'll never have any. If I had a child, I'd never, *ever* let him get into danger. Or her.'

The hailstones are huge and cold. They hurt my face and polka-dot Deirdre's black coat. I can hardly see.

'Look,' I shout, over the wind. 'We've got to get out of this weather. Come on.'

I grab her by the arm and pull her along with me back the way we came, then down to the streets below the bridge. By luck more than good sense, I find the Bridge Café, where it always was, at the corner of Dover Street and Water Street.

It's a huge relief to ease through the door of the old building into the warm interior. The place is just as I remember: small and tranquil, tables set with tablecloths and napkins, good smells of soup and stew. Behind the dark wooden bar counter a bartender pours yellow Galliano into a tall glass. A waiter smiles and waves us to a small table in the corner. The place is half-empty. I look at the antique clock above the bar and it's 2.25 p.m.

'Are you still serving lunch?' I ask.

'We sure are, sir,' says the waiter and places two menus on our table.

Deirdre takes off her damp coat and hat, and I hang them next to my parka on the old-fashioned coat rack. We settle into our chairs.

'This is supposed to be the oldest business establishment in New York,' I say. 'It was a brothel originally, back in the nineteenth century.'

'I'm sorry,' she says as she fishes a tissue out of her shoulder bag. She wipes her eyes. 'I lost it a bit, didn't I?'

'Ah, don't worry,' I say.

'Look,' she says. 'Do you want children?'

'Not really.' I pick up a menu and I don't see the words. Instead, the background music registers in my brain. I know the song: 'The Ballad of the Sad Young Men'. Sylvia used to play it. Ricki Lee Jones is a great vocalist, but on this song her voice is full of tears. She sings of sad young men, choking on their youth. I can't hear the rest because Deirdre leans across the table and the way she's looking at me demands my complete attention.

'Are you sure?' she says.

'Yeah.'

'Have you ever wanted kids?'

The waiter comes over. I pick the first thing I see on the menu.

'I'll have the Crispy Chicken Sandwich,' I say.

'Me too.' That's the quickest decision Deirdre's ever made in my experience, except when she buys shoes.

'Drinks?' asks the waiter.

'It's my birthday. We'll have some Cava, something like that. What do you reckon?'

'We have a nice medium dry Prosecco, sir.'

'That'll do fine, won't it, Deirdre?'

'Yes.'

The waiter walks away.

'I can't have any,' says Deirdre.

'Sure you can. Have a glass, anyway. It'll do you good.'

'I'll have some wine, it's not wine I'm talking about. It's kids. I can't have any kids.'

'Oh.'

'That's what I've been trying to tell you. I had Stage IV endometriosis. It's a disease of the womb. I was in agony every month...'

'Oh no,' I say, horrified. 'Don't tell me the details. You know I can't bear to hear about women's stuff.'

'I'm just telling you what happened; I'm trying to *explain*...'

'Okay, I'm listening.'

'Well, I tried shovelling painkillers down my throat, more and more of them, but it only got worse and I ended up in hospital. They put me on some medicine for six months, the same stuff they use to treat blokes with testicular cancer. It was terrible — made me really depressed. Didn't work either.'

'So?'

She looks at me, hard. 'You're not even interested, are you?'

'Jesus!' I say. 'Of course I am. Go on.'

'The consultant said I needed a hysterectomy. I said "no way". I tried Chinese medicine. I'd heard it could work wonders, but it was disgusting. I couldn't stand the taste of it. So I gave up.'

I don't know what to say, so I look at her with an expression I hope is interested and alert.

'Well,' she continues, looking at me and then down at the table. 'After a few weeks I went back to the consultant and said, "I give up. Take the whole damn lot out. Just do it." So he did. That was three years ago.'

She looks older than her twenty-nine years now.

'I should have taken that herbal medicine,' she adds. 'I met a woman last week who went to the same Chinese doctor for seven months and she's fine now.'

I feel a bit dazed. I thought Deirdre was different. I didn't realise she was so much like me; the kind of person who gives up on things far too easily.

'So that's it,' she says. 'I'll never have any children.'

The wine arrives, and as soon as the waiter has filled our glasses I raise mine.

'Well,' I say. 'Cheers.'

'Happy birthday. Sorry for the tears and all that.'

'It's fine. You gave the taxi driver a bit of a shock, but it won't do him any harm.'

'Loads of crappy people who shouldn't have children end up

having heaps of them,' she says in a shaky voice. 'And some people who would be fantastic parents can't conceive at all.'

My drunken words of last night are coming back to me. I should be able to say them again. I should tell her about the snip too, but I just sit here and say nothing.

'Disappointment,' she says. 'It's a highly under-rated emotion, you know.'

The plates of food arrive and we both look down at them.

I don't know why I can't tell her.

That night I lie awake next to Deirdre. She smells so fresh and clean even when she's asleep; it must be that expensive body lotion that she uses. I should be able to sleep easy now. I always thought Deirdre would dump me so she could have kids with some other guy. Problem over. I can relax now, can't I?

But I can't seem to relax. I haven't told Deirdre about the snip. Why didn't I tell her straight away? Maybe I should wake her up now and tell her the good news. I imagine how I'll say it. *Guess what? I can't have kids either, so we're quits!* But Deirdre has got cranky in the past when I've woken her up with one of my bright ideas, so I think better of it. Instead, I begin to imagine our future life together.

Deirdre and I will have a dog, I think. A little terrier. I always wanted a dog. The ideal dog flashes in my brain; a German Schnauzer, a black and white one, called... called Spike. Of course we'll have to sell my studio flat and Deirdre's tiny house in Prosperity Square, because we'll need a decent garden for the dog. I see us in a townhouse somewhere near the Lee Fields so we can stride out with Spike and take him for long twice-daily walks along the river. The scenes rush along in my head: Spike running towards me, tongue lolling, tail wagging, across Inchydoney Strand; Spike dozing in his dog basket while I sit at my desk and write; Deirdre and I watching TV together, the dog sitting between us on the couch; Spike pelting out into the hall when he hears the key in the lock, because he knows it's Deirdre arriving home from work.

I'm half-awake, half-dreaming, when a second scenario starts up in my head. Deirdre and I are older now, and we're walking in a park but we have no dog. Somehow, I know that Spike the dog is dead. We walk past a busy playground and Deirdre halts. I say 'Come on, slowcoach,' but she makes no reply. She just stands there, looking bitter, as she stares at other people's children.

The dreamlike scene shifts. Now, we're at a dinner party. Suddenly, Deirdre clatters her knife and fork down on her plate and insists on telling everyone loudly that neither of us can have children. It is her deepest regret, she says. Someone says there are ways and means but Deirdre says 'shut up' and then starts raging again like she did in the yellow cab. I make our excuses and drag her away. She snarls at me in a long mirrored hall, her face like a puppet in a Punch and Judy Show, and I wake from the nightmare in horror, her words still turning in my head: *Disappointment is an under-rated emotion.*

Feverish now, and wide awake, another thought enters my head. Deirdre can't have children. What if I actually *can*? I never considered getting the operation reversed. Maybe it's possible? What if I did and it worked? What if I could have children *and* a dog?

Careful not to wake Deirdre, I get out of bed and fumble in the dark until I find my iPad. I sneak into the bathroom and close the door before turning on the light, so the noise of the extractor fan won't wake her. Once I'm inside I fumble for the light and turn it on. I settle down on the toilet seat and begin googling.

When I type in 'Successful vasectomy reversals', I find an article in the *Daily News* about a bloke called Harry who reversed his. He had the snip about ten years ago, same as myself, and now his second wife, Lola, age twenty-nine, is expecting their first baby. A guy called Aaron tells a similar story on his blog. Why did I never consider this before? Getting unsnipped seems like a good idea now. I check out a few more blogs before sneaking quietly back to bed.

It's two days since we got back to Cork. I'm sitting in the Pavilion Bar waiting for Deirdre. She's late. I've almost finished my Americano when she comes in.

'What would you like?' I ask.

'Nothing,' she says. 'I can't stay long.' She sits next to me and puts her hand on my arm. 'Look, someone has to say it, so I will. We're going to break up, aren't we?' she says. She takes her arm from mine and places both her hands in her lap, one minding the other.

'No, no, no,' I say. 'Come on, where's all this coming from?'

'Don't pretend. Please don't. You wanted to break up with me when we were in New York. I could see it in your face. I'm just making it easier for you.'

I feel ashamed.

'It's because I can't have children,' she continues. 'I'm damaged goods, even for you.'

I wonder what she means when she says 'even for you,' but I don't ask.

'To be fair, you never said you loved me — except that one time in New York, the night you were really drunk. Still, for a while, I really thought we could make a go of it.'

I almost say something but I don't know what to say.

She looks as if she's about to cry. She stands up. 'Don't worry. It's not your fault. I'll get over it.' She tries to smile at me. It's a brave half-smile. 'I'll manage. Who knows? I might even get myself a little terrier to keep me company.'

And then she's gone. The waiter comes over and asks if I want anything else.

'I don't know what I want,' I say as I stare at my empty cup.

HOUSEWIFE OF THE YEAR

I love cleaning. I have to clean the floor right now. But I can talk to you while I clean, can't I?

My mother was 'Housewife of the Year' in 1966. Forty years ago, that was. She'd be seventy now if she was still alive.

Oh, it was a big competition. Everyone said she'd never come first. You needed about eight children to win, no matter how good you were at housewifely stuff, and she had only five. I was the youngest, just four at the time. You really had to have babies and young kids hanging off you, left, right and centre, to be a winner. But my father died suddenly, soon after she posted the entry form. She was a widow then; that balanced things out.

It was as if they weighed the entrants on an old-fashioned weighing scale. You know the kind — the ones you see under Libra in horoscopes. On the shiny metal bowl on the left-hand side you'd have a smiling attractive lady with a perfect hairdo, the kind you could tell was hard-won from gritty curlers left in overnight. She'd be posing like a model, with long stockinged legs. But instead of a designer outfit she'd be wearing a beautiful home-tailored housecoat or apron, ironed to perfection, with a sign saying, 'I can bake and sew and look fabulous, in spite of all this'. Cooker and washing machine and hoover and mop all piled in behind her, with an arrow pointing to the other side of the scales. On the other bowl all the kids would be piled in along with their bikes and footballs, loads of them. The children would have signs around their necks saying, 'We go to Mass every Sunday in our best clothes'; 'We speak Irish fluently'; 'We take piano lessons'; 'We learn Irish dancing'; 'We play Gaelic games'. My mother won and I realised that having only five children was enough if you could lob a coffin marked 'Dead Husband' into the scales on the kid side.

My mother was as bitter as the lemon juice she liked to drink in a glass of warm water. It was to keep her skin good. It didn't make her temper any better. Sometimes I thought I'd crumble and fade away with the shouting.

'You dirty scut... you little scumbag...'

She complained about my behaviour, told me I was good for nothing. She said I looked like a tinker when my socks didn't match the ribbon in my hair. Nothing was good enough. I never answered back. The children in our house were human mice.

To discourage any rodent from entering your house, use spearmint or peppermint essential oils either in water or in alcohol. Fifteen to twenty percent in alcohol is the strongest formulation. Place strategically around the house and roof. This should discourage them from turning your residence into theirs.

My mother made the best brown bread. When she won prizes at the annual ICA competitions, she was pleased, and there was peace in the house for a while.

But I liked Mrs Flynn's bread better. Mrs Flynn was disorganised. She didn't enter any competitions and her hair fell in wisps from underneath her scarf, but she was very cheery and didn't seem to notice crumbs.

'Oh God, I'm not able to do anything fancy!' she said. 'Only plain aul' cooking… stews an' that sort of thing. Isn't your mother a wonder! Sure she's "Cor-dong Blue" qualified an' all, isn't she?'

When my father died, my mother took over the family business — a hardware shop on Main Street. She had two shop assistants, but she was in charge. We had to help out of course, on Saturdays, after school and during the holidays. She baked and cleaned and darned and ironed when she wasn't in the shop. And she entered the competition.

We could hardly believe it when we saw her on the *Late Late Show*. There she was, one of six finalists, cooking a three-course meal on TV. Gaybo shook her hand and shook his head, said she was Wonderwoman. She told him our names and smiled as if she really loved us. We believed it because it was on TV. We were hysterical when the winner was announced at the end of the show. Gaybo put his arm around her shoulders and somebody gave her a huge bunch of flowers. Mrs Flynn was minding us for the weekend. She jumped up and down, cheering at the television. She hugged all of us, her face red with excitement.

Everyone came out to welcome my mother home, as if she was the whole GAA team wrapped together in one. A newspaper man and a photographer came to the house. Mrs Flynn was in a terrible rush to get us all into our Sunday best for the photo. My mother's recipes for 'Beef in Beer Stew' and 'Lemon Candy Biscuits', ones she invented for the competition, were published in the *Cork Examiner* and in the *Southern Star*, with photos and a report. We were in a photo too. We were famous.

... Cook in a low oven (140°C) for two and a half hours. Don't lift the lid and have a taste halfway through. The delicious sauce needs time to develop and must be left alone ...

Tom left home first, to London, as a labourer. Marie went over next, to do nursing. They managed to save a few bob and went from there to America. The twins, Jim and Grace, worked all the hours God sent while they were in secondary school and somehow saved enough money to get a real distance between themselves and home as soon as they could; they ended up in Australia. None of them wanted to come back.

'*You're* not going anywhere,' my mother said to me. 'I need someone to help in the shop.'

I got my Leaving Cert results. They were better than I'd expected. It took all my courage to apply for a clerical job in the Civil Service. I posted the application secretly. When I went to Dublin for the entrance exam, I told her I was going to Cork to buy a winter coat. I was called for an interview and I made up another lie. The job offer came in a brown envelope. She found it, read it out loud to me.

'You ungrateful little bitch. There's no way you're leaving me here on my own.'

She frightened me but I packed my bags and left, anyhow.

Dublin was grand. That's where I met Sean. Strong, dark, a hard worker. He sang, too, when he had a few drinks taken. No one in my family sang. I'd never known his kind of singing—only hymns in church.

I remember the first weekend I spent with him in the Sheedy Falls Hotel. We hardly left the bedroom. We couldn't keep our hands off each other.

Mrs Flynn rang me. 'She's not well. Could you get a few days off? I didn't know who else to contact.'

Going back was the last thing I wanted to do, but Sean couldn't understand.

'She's your mother,' he said.

'I suppose you're right,' I agreed. I didn't want him to think badly of me.

My mother was in bed, looking feeble. For a few seconds I thought I could see a shadow of gratitude in her eyes. I was wrong.

'What are *you* doing here?' she said. And then, 'Well, since you're back you might as well make yourself useful.'

She was my real mother again and I finally gave up my secret hope that some day she would love me.

I did my best. I made invalid food and cleaned out the fridge and washed the floors and talked to the staff in the shop. I didn't answer my mother back. I managed not to explode when she screeched orders from upstairs.

When you replace that little box of baking soda in your fridge with a fresh one twice a year, don't let the old one go to waste. Pour it down the drain and chase it with half a cup of white vinegar. You'll create a small chemical reaction, a little volcano that will naturally clean and freshen the drain.

'I have a life, you know,' I said, one night, as I set the regulation night-time mug of cocoa carefully on her bedside cabinet. 'I have a relationship.' I hadn't realised until I said it out loud that I really did have a relationship.

'What's his name? What does he do?' she said, from the mustiness of her bed.

I told her. 'He'll be here on Friday.'

'He can have Tom's room,' she said.

'No need. He'll come in with me,' I replied.

'You little tramp,' she said in a thin voice.

I'd underestimated her. Just because she was bedridden with some inexplicable illness didn't make her less vicious.

'You filthy trollop. You can't have a man in your room. And of course you can't go back. You must *mind* me. After all I did for you. All the cleaning and cooking, all the work I put in. You great big strap, you'll do as you're told.'

I put a pillow over her head instead of under it.

I heard Mrs Flynn in the street that night. It was pub-closing time and she was singing *Moon River*, loudly. She pressed the doorbell too long.

'Is something wrong?' she asked, anxiously, leaning on Mr Flynn's arm. 'We saw the lights on. Has she had a bad turn?'

I was wearing my mother's housecoat, the one with small pink roses on a blue background. I'd always liked that one best. A pair of rubber gloves, yellow marigolds, to protect my hands.

'My mother's dead,' I said. I hadn't been planning to announce it so soon.

Mr Flynn insisted on calling the police.

I hated the undertaker. The odd 'not really a smile' version of a smile on his face. His son looked about ten years old and he was dressed up in a black suit and a miniature top hat, just like his father. What were they playing at? The child should be a page boy if anything and there he was at the church looking like a goblin undertaker.

Only my brother Jim made it home for the funeral. His twin, Grace, sent me a note. None of them sent Mass Cards. I wondered why we were all so scattered. When I saw Jim I realised how much I missed them all. He only stayed a few days.

'Sorry, Sis,' he said. He'd become very Australian. 'Can't hack it over here.'

Sean was great. He proposed to me not long after the funeral and I accepted. I was twenty-nine and it was time. We couldn't get enough of each other then. I wore white and my going-away outfit was black.

Sean set himself up as a property developer and worked hard. The Celtic Tiger purred. We sold the hardware shop. I made sure my brothers and sisters got their share and I put my own money in the Credit Union.

We wanted children so badly for a while. I can't think why, it must have been Sean who wanted them. I would have found the dirt difficult. Nappies I wouldn't really mind. Disposable ones, I mean. You just take them off, throw them away, put on a clean one. It's all the other stuff, trawling in dirt on their shoes, crumbs, spills. I wouldn't like that. Cuts, grazes, no. I wouldn't mind the extra laundry. I love doing laundry.

Remove perspiration stains and odour from clothing by applying a paste of baking soda and water and letting it soak for 30 minutes prior to laundering.

'Don't despair,' said Sean. 'Give up work. Maybe that will help.'

I did. For a while I spent all my time in the gym and at the shops. I had lots of clothes, make-up and jewelry. Regular visits to the hairdresser. An occasional manicure. I kept everything spotless for when my perfect husband came home. A casserole in the oven. Ironed sheets.

Keep raw eggs fresh in the refrigerator by applying a light coat of solid vegetable shortening. The shortening seals the egg, which keeps the air out and helps the egg to last longer.

I kept a clean house. No one can say anything against me on that score. I don't know why Sean had to interfere.

'We'll get a maid,' he said. 'I'm worried about you. I didn't mean you to leave work only to become a house slave. I meant you to have a good life.'

He insisted on hiring someone to do the cleaning. She was from Maldavia, somewhere like that. One of those Russian places. I tried to be nice to her.

'Do you like cleaning?' I asked.

She spoke English in a glutinous way. 'I pretend like it's my house,' she said in her odd foreign accent. 'Then I laike.'

I didn't like her tone.

She told me she needed more cleaning cloths and I got them. She liked my feather duster and wanted another. I got two in Eurobuster in North Main Street. And for good measure, I got an extendable Vileda mop.

I had to go out while she cleaned. She gave me the evil eye if I watched her. It was odd. She reminded me of someone but I couldn't place her.

One day I came home early. It was lunchtime. Sean was in the kitchen, eating a sandwich and talking to the cleaner.

'So if you had €12,000 you could buy a house back home?' he was saying.

'I can get gut house even for less.'

'How many bedrooms would you get for that kind of money? Oh, hello love! I decided to come home for my lunch.'

'Oh.'

'This good lady here made me a lovely sandwich.'

I checked her cleaning. Not good enough. Not up to standard. I tried not to think about it. Inside me, something screamed.

The last time she cleaned, the taps in the washbasins were shining, but between the chrome taps and the white enamel there was a brownish-yellow edge, like a thin line of mustard. Revolting. She should have gone right in there with a J-cloth.

When I lifted the cushions of the leather settees, I was raging. Balls of dust underneath. A €1 coin and the ring pull from a can of lager. An empty packet of Tayto crisps. One of my hoop earrings. How could she be so careless? She was scrubbing the kitchen floor when I stabbed her. It was dead hard to move her and it took ages to clean up afterwards. She was found three days later in Farren Wood. I didn't even know her surname until I saw it in the paper.

I overheard Sean talking to our neighbour.

'She never stops cleaning,' he said. 'What on earth am I going to do, Sue? I'm really worried about her. It's only getting worse.'

'Maybe she hasn't got over her mother's death,' said Sue.

I know her type. That bitch couldn't care less.

'And of course that murder of the poor foreign girl who was cleaning for you — that must have given her an awful shock.'

'She got the newest Dyson a month ago,' he said. 'There wasn't a thing wrong with the old one. She trades up in vacuum cleaners like they're cars.'

'Have you asked her to go for counselling, at all?'

'I have, but not a hope. She says I should go for counselling myself, that it's my problem.'

Don't think I don't know what that hussy wants. She wants to get me locked up so she can take my husband away from me.

'Well, if there's anything I can do…?'

'No, nothing, I'm afraid. She wasn't always like this, you know. I'll just have to hope for the best.'

The dirty whore. And he's falling for it, too, for her dirty plans. I know he is.

I don't want to do it with him any more. Once upon a time I couldn't get enough. I can't believe I was interested in sex. It's all so... so dirty, so filthy. Once upon a time I used to take it in my mouth. Sixty-nine. Three or four times a day. We did it whenever we got the chance. Nothing else, only food, drink and the two of us.

That weekend at the Sheedy Falls Hotel; it must have happened to two other people who looked just like us. 'Fuck me, fuck me hard.' How did I have the time to wash everything, including myself? I don't understand. All those bodily fluids; it makes me retch to think of it now.

I can't bear the smell of his sweat. I have to change the sheets right after he does it to me. Unbearable to sleep in all that sweatiness; and the wet patch appalls me. Once he cried and the pillow was all wet, so wet I had to throw it out. He went to the spare room after that. More cleaning, of course, but sure what does he care? He trawls in with muddy boots from tramping round the country buying more and more land and making more and more money. He's not crying any more though. He looked at me in a puzzled kind of way for a while. He's stopped doing that now.

'I can't live like this,' he said. 'Not any more. I'm leaving you.'

Bloodstains: Three percent hydrogen peroxide is super for removing bloodstains. It's also a great bleaching agent for stubborn stains on white clothes. Combine half a cup of hydrogen peroxide and one teaspoon of ammonia for an unbeatable stain removal combination. Just make sure to use three percent and not the kind you use to bleach your hair.

'Who the hell do you think you are?' he said. 'Housewife of the Year?'

He shouldn't have said that.

A GOOD FUNERAL

Luke's father lies in a hospital bed in a private room. Luke stands at the foot of the bed, holding a bunch of oriental lilies he bought at Cork airport. Their scent is muted in the antiseptic hospital air.

His brother Terence and Terence's wife Una sit at the old man's bedside in a silence broken by the click of the morphine pump, then a clatter of crockery and muffled voices from the corridor outside. The old man seems dead already, until suddenly his blue eyes flicker open.

'If you've come to get something out of me, forget it,' he manages to say.

'That's not why I came,' says Luke. The tremor in his own voice reminds him of the child he once was.

The old man closes his eyes and seems to sleep. Two nurses come in.

'Sorry to disturb you,' the older nurse says. 'We need a few minutes.'

'I'll put those flowers in water for you,' the younger one offers.

In the corridor Luke takes a deep breath. 'Jesus,' he says. 'He's not

changed much, has he? After twenty-five years that's all he has to say
to me.'

'I didn't think he was able to talk any more,' says Terence.

'Me neither,' says Una. 'We might as well have a bite to eat, while
the nurses are sorting him out.'

They go to the hospital cafeteria. While Luke eats a limp salad
sandwich and drinks bitter coffee, Terence and Una share a pot of tea,
and the old man dies, alone.

'What are your plans?' asks Terence, later.

'I have no plans,' Luke answers. 'After I got your phone call, I just
packed a bag and left.'

'I'm sorry, but you can't stay with us,' says Una.

Luke looks at her, tries to stay calm. He knows how Bernard
would describe Una, if he were still alive. *A good breeder but a bad
egg.* He misses Bernard so much that sometimes he can't breathe.

'I'm not being funny,' Una adds. 'But you'd only stress Terence out
and I've enough on my plate right now, to be honest.' She has retained
the sturdy good looks of her youth but she seems tougher now, in her
well-applied make-up and expensive clothes.

'Me, stress Terence out? Let's face it, *I* never gave Terence a hard
time for being *straight*, did I?'

Una says nothing. The grim expression on her face reminds him
of a long-ago incident. She had tried to kiss him once outside the
local disco back home in Atharnavar—she must have been sixteen
then—and she's glaring at him now just as she did when he rebuffed
her, all those years ago.

Terence breaks the awkward silence.

'Ah, it's just... with the kids and all... I was only thinking you'd
have more peace if you stayed in the old man's place,' he says,
apologetically, and hands over a set of keys.

When Luke inserts the Yale key in the front door of the old homestead,
it won't turn at first. He jiggles it helplessly for a moment and curses

quietly. Then he remembers the trick of it. He grasps the door knob and pulls the front door towards him while he turns the key. This time there's a click and it opens.

The hall is dark and forbidding, an immediate and confusing contrast to the June brightness outside, and it smells of dry rot and tobacco.

In the sitting room, an ashtray full of butts overflows on the mantelpiece and yellowing antimacassars embroidered by Luke's late mother still clothe the armchairs. The shelves on each side of the fireplace are half-empty and two cardboard boxes full of books sit on the floor next to them.

Luke walks through the sitting room into the kitchen, where a solitary mug sits upturned on the draining board. Drawers and cupboard doors are half open and cardboard boxes filled with crockery and cutlery sit on the worktops. His chest feels tight and he opens the back door to breathe.

The garden is almost as he remembers it, just smaller and more unkempt. A concrete yard, a bit of dried-up lawn, gaunt gooseberry bushes, a lopsided clothesline, the stooping crab-apple tree, a new wooden shed. The doorbell rings, and he turns back to answer it.

A man in jeans and patterned shirt stands outside, a black bin bag in each hand. He is slim and has an angular lightly freckled face. He's probably in his mid-thirties.

'Una sent me over,' he announces. 'It's clean bedding.'

'Thank you.'

'You're welcome.' He moves past Luke and puts the bags down in the hallway. Then he turns and says, 'Sorry about your dad. It must be tough, coming home to this.'

'We weren't exactly what you'd call close, but... yeah, it's a bit weird.'

'I'm Jamie by the way—the youngest of the Mannings. I was only fourteen or fifteen the last time you were here.'

'Gosh, that was a long time ago—1984, I think. I only stayed two days.' Luke pauses. 'I remember you now. You were always asking me for cigarettes, weren't you?'

'Yeah, and I never got any from you. You told me I was too young to be smoking.'

'You were, too,' grins Luke. 'So... have you always lived here?'

'No way. Hell, no.' Jamie's still standing in the hall. He leans against the wall near the stairs and pats the front pockets of his jeans as if he's searching for cigarettes. 'I'm in engineering but I got laid off recently so I rented my gaff in Dublin and came back home for a while.'

'Oh.'

'It's okay. I've a job lined up in Dubai, so I'll be off as soon as my visa arrives.' He finds a pack of ten Marlboro Lights in the top pocket of his shirt, along with a Bic lighter. He offers the cigarettes to Luke, who shakes his head.

'No, thanks — but you go ahead.'

'You sure?'

Luke nods so Jamie lights up and exhales. 'You used to work in the pub yourself, didn't you?' he says.

'I did. The weekends were mad busy. Is it still the same?'

'It's hectic on a Saturday night, but quiet enough during the week. The wine bar upstairs is doing okay, I think, since they got a Spanish chef in to do tapas a few months ago.'

'Really? I didn't know it was a wine bar now.'

'Did they not show you round?'

'No. No they didn't.'

'Actually, that reminds me. Una's on her way down, so I better head. She'll be bitching if I stop to chat.'

'Will she?'

'Ah, you know the way,' Jamie says. 'It's been nice talking to you. See you later.' He walks away with a swing to his hips and a backward glance that seems to Luke astonishingly like an invitation.

Luke watches Jamie until he disappears round the corner at the end of the street. He's about to go back inside when he sees Una coming from the same direction. She's carrying a Dunnes Stores' bag and looks tired. Luke remembers Terence talking about her when he was seventeen. She was a 'ride', he had said. Luke had been shocked at the dismissive words.

'I brought a few provisions,' she says, handing him the bag.

'Would you like to come in?'

'No,' she answers. 'I've enough of this place. Always in and out to make sure he was alright and not a word of thanks for it.'

'He was never easy.'

Una stands there, silent.

'There'll be no settlement,' she says then, sharply. 'Just in case you think there will be.'

'I didn't think anything.'

'It's alright for you,' she continues. 'You escaped. You had the high life in London. We had to stay here. We're the ones had to put up with him. We deserve something for that.'

'Look, I'll be gone as soon as the funeral's over. I know he's left me nothing. I don't care.'

'That's alright so,' she relents. 'Sure you're not the worst in the world, are you?'

'Are you planning to sell this place?' asks Luke. 'Someone's been packing stuff, so I wondered.'

Una avoids his eyes. 'Ah, I was just doing a bit of tidying while I had the chance,' she says. 'We might rent it out for a while.' She turns to leave. 'Oh, I nearly forgot… the removal is at seven tomorrow evening and the "afters" will be in our own pub.'

'And the funeral?'

'That's at two, the following day. You'll have to be at the church at about half one, I'd say. There'll be a meal in the hotel afterwards— we're expecting about two hundred.'

'Fine.'

There's a brand-new double divan in the room that was once Luke's bedroom. He tears the plastic covering off and puts the fitted sheet on the mattress, then places the pillows and duvet on top. There's nothing familiar about his old bedroom except its shape and size, and the view from the window, where evening sun is stretching now across the back yard. It was June when Bernard died, too, but Luke does not remember any sun that year.

He goes downstairs and contemplates his mobile phone. His therapist has advised him that grieving is a slow process and that he must not isolate himself, so Luke contemplates ringing his friend Colette in London. He finds her number but changes his mind. Instead, he puts the mobile phone down on the old dining table and rubs his forehead with his hands. *Why can't I cry for Bernard?* he wonders. *Why can't I cry? I wish I could have said goodbye to him. A proper goodbye. I love you, goodbye.*

Luke decides to leave the house for a while. As he walks past the pub, he sees about a dozen people outside, smoking. He nods at them, wishing for a moment that he still smoked. Jamie is at the side door. As he looks up from lighting a cigarette, he sees Luke.

'Hi,' he smiles. 'Having a break. Don't tell Una.'

'I won't.'

'Or Terence.'

'No.'

'Cigarette?'

'I'm tempted, but no thanks.'

'It must be hard for you, being back.'

'It is,' Luke admits. 'I never fitted in.'

'Me neither. What are you up to?'

'Nothing. I don't know what to do with myself, to be honest.'

'Pity I'm working tonight. Do you want to come for a spin tomorrow? I'm off until five. I could call to you around midday?'

Luke hesitates.

'I'll get you back here in good time.'

There is a hint of yearning in Jamie's voice that makes Luke suspect that he's not merely flirtatious — that he's lonely, too.

'Sounds good.'

'Brilliant.' Jamie looks at his watch. 'Jeez, I'd better go or there'll be war. I'll see you tomorrow, so.'

In the morning, Jamie pulls up outside the house in an old yellow convertible with the hood down.

'Yeah, it's a Triumph Stag,' he says, when Luke admires the car. '1974. I'm a bit of a petrol-head, to be honest.'

As Jamie points out, it's rare to have a good forecast in Ireland, even in June, and today is going to be sunny, so they might as well make the most of it. Jamie's a good driver and soon Luke begins to relax, though it's hard to talk above the sound of the engine and the wind whipping around his head.

'Music?' Jamie asks.

'Sure,' says Luke.

A lead is attached to the cassette that Jamie pushes into the tape deck and the other end of the lead clicks into Jamie's iPod. It looks odd, but it works.

'That's clever,' shouts Luke, his words almost lost in the breeze.

Soon they're in the countryside, where purple-pink foxgloves stand among ferns and briars along the narrow roads. Luke and Jamie sing along to 'Do You Know the Way to San José?' but then, above the sound of the engine, Luke recognises the next song, 'Missing' by Tracey Thorn, and he feels a familiar ache in his chest.

Bernard was a hopeless driver but he loved being driven, and Luke is filled with regret that he never drove Bernard along these roads, that Bernard never saw these fields, these clouds, these foxgloves, the red fuchsia, those clumps of orange montbretia, this green place.

'Here we are,' says Jamie, parking in front of a small pub almost hidden behind trees. They sit in the beer-garden with glasses of cider and toasted cheese sandwiches. They talk of Luke's advertising agency in London, of Jamie's future job in Dubai, of cars and wine and pleasure, and not a word about pain.

In the funeral parlour that evening, Luke keeps as far away from the coffin as he can. It's warm and there's a strange smell. He feels faint and wonders if it's the embalming fluid. Terence and Una stand near him. People approach, single file, to shake hands and tell him they are sorry for his troubles. They know nothing about his troubles.

The final sympathiser is gently ushered out of the room by the priest, who says, 'Let's give the family some private time,' and closes the door. Terence and Una bow their heads as if in prayer, while Luke moves closer to the coffin to take a last look at his father's chalky face. A wave of grey hair has been gelled and carefully combed over one side of the dead man's high forehead and Luke wonders who had the courage to take such a liberty. Indeed, the old man looks irritable, even in death.

Bernard's face in death was pale and immobile too. Luke forces himself to remember Bernard when he was alive instead... He remembers a night when Bernard wore nothing but his extra-large Calvin Klein underpants and a pink party wig while he moon-walked very badly, singing 'Billie Jean', the two of them howling with laughter. All Luke wants to do now is howl in pain.

In the church, repetitious prayers are half-said. The coffin has been brought here from the funeral parlour where it will stay overnight until the funeral Mass tomorrow. Luke kneels in a front pew with Terence and Una. The kneelers are cushioned in soft green leather but Luke remembers his knees aching on wooden boards when he was a child. Other memories come... sitting in the pew behind pious Mrs Conway, the delightful agony of seeing a 'fat pig' crawling along the light brown fur of her mink stole during a long sermon, waiting for the inexorable drop of the insect into the space between the woman's neck and the fur. His own mother wore a black mantilla in those days. She was a gentle but ineffectual woman who failed to shield him from his father's distaste. She died when Luke was twenty and her funeral was much like this one, all Catholic formality and incense, hymns sung in faint voices over the bellicose organ.

Bernard's funeral had been quite different: a Humanist service in Golders Green crematorium, and afterwards, invited guests for excellent food and wine in Claridge's. A string quartet played Bach, while hastily-assembled scrapbooks containing photographs and mementoes were passed round, summoning memories of parties, holidays, private views at Bernard's gallery and picnics at Kenwood House.

'He'd have liked his funeral,' a friend had observed, but Luke didn't know. He hadn't had a chance to ask. Bernard had suffered a too-early heart attack and Luke could only guess what he might have wanted. Since the funeral Luke has lived alone in their house in Highgate. He has changed nothing in the house and is still in therapy.

To thee do we cry poor banished children of Eve,
To thee do we send up our sighs,
mourning and weeping in this valley of tears...

The removal is finally over. Outside, Luke overhears a stout woman talking in a low knowing voice to a smaller lady in a beige coat.

'They say he went very quick in the end... jus' like that,' she says. Luke suddenly has a vision of the late comedian Tommy Cooper wearing a fez, and almost laughs. He wishes Bernard was still alive, so that he could recount it all to him later, knowing Bernard would get all the nuances. A sudden sharp pain in his chest makes him think for a minute that he might be dying himself, though his consultant has run tests and assured him there's nothing physically wrong with him.

In the pub, there are refreshments for the mourners. Girls in white shirts and navy suits offer trays of sherry and serve tea and coffee, sandwiches and cake. Jamie is busy behind the bar but he smiles at Luke across the room when he notices him. The stout lady and her friend tell Luke they wouldn't recognise him after all these years and that the sandwiches are delicious.

Luke goes out for air. As he stands outside the back door of the pub, Jamie emerges and lights a cigarette.

'How's it going?' he asks.

'It's... weird. Thanks for the drive, by the way. Cleared my head a bit.'

'It's the least I can do. You're my hero, you know.'

'What?'

'Well, you were the first person I ever knew who was "out". You went around looking like Bowie, no compromise, like. Myself and my pal Don — we were well-impressed.'

'You're joking.' But Luke feels warmed.

Next day, Luke stands with his brother in the vestibule of the church before the funeral Mass begins.

Terence looks sideways at him and Luke wonders if his dark pinstripe suit is wrong for the occasion, or if the pale blue pattern of his shirt is at odds with the black tie Terence has lent him.

'What's wrong?' he says.

'Nothing,' says Terence.

'No, say it.'

'For fuck's sake, Luke, just act normal, will you? Just this once?'

Again, today, people come up to Luke and say, 'You don't remember me, do you?' A portly man with a ruddy face and dark hair says, 'Sorry for your troubles, Terence,' and shakes his hand briskly, then turns to Luke. 'It's yourself,' he says. 'You don't know me at all, do you?'

'No,' says Luke evenly. But he remembers Hoggy very well — a boy who had lain in wait for him after school, then wrestled him to the ground near the quiet river walk and writhed on top of him, panting, 'Go on, cry away, you little Mammy's boy,' before cuffing him around the head and letting him go. Luke feels like taking Hoggy outside and grinding his face into the churchyard gravel. Instead, he says, 'I haven't a clue who you are.' The man frowns and moves off, into the dim light of the church.

'There was no need for that,' Terence hisses.

More people arrive. More smiles. More handshakes. Luke's hand begins to ache. The undertaker tells them it's time to go inside.

The concelebrated Mass takes forever. There are eulogies for a man that Luke doesn't recognise: a great GAA supporter, a man who ran a fine bar and gave employment to many. Finally, one of the priests walks round the coffin shaking incense and then holy water. Terence and Luke link arms, and with four other men they carry the coffin awkwardly out of the church and lower it into the back of the hearse. People shuffle away. Car doors slam.

'Aren't we going to walk behind the coffin?' Luke asks. 'That's what we did at Mam's funeral.'

Una looks annoyed. 'For God's sake, no one does that any more. How long is it since *you've* been to a funeral?'

Luke doesn't bother to reply. A black car takes them to the graveside where the final prayers are said and the coffin is lowered into the grave.

In the hotel there is a sit-down meal of vegetable soup, then a choice of beef or salmon with mash and peas. Luke wonders if anyone has remembered that he's vegetarian. He takes a spoonful of the vegetable soup and tastes chicken stock.

The woman sitting next to Luke is, apparently, a distant relative, and has a kind face. She says she knew his mother well, God rest her soul.

'Yes,' he answers her question. 'I'm only home for the funeral.'

He excuses himself and goes to the Gents. As he sits on the lid of the toilet in one of the cubicles, he hears two men come in.

'A grand spread,' says one voice. 'I won't need to ate for a few days after this.'

They both laugh and piss noisily in the urinals.

The second man says, 'Sure a good funeral is better than a bad wedding, any day, as the fella says.'

They laugh again and talk a little more while clothing is being adjusted. Soon the door bangs behind them and they're gone. Luke quickly leaves the Gents. He walks out of the hotel and over to the pub. It's almost empty today, just two young men playing pool. Jamie is the only barman to be seen.

'A double whiskey please,' says Luke.

'Getting a bit too much for you, is it?' asks Jamie.

'It is. Some things are different here but, underneath, nothing's really changed.'

'I know exactly what you mean. At least you'll be out of here soon.' He moves away to serve an old man who's standing at the counter, then comes back to Luke.

'Do you want some company later on?'

Luke hesitates. 'I'm... I'm not much fun right now,' he says.

'Look, I'm off at seven. I'll call over, see how you're feeling.'

Luke wanders towards the hotel. He meets Una outside. She's smoking a cigarette, shifting from one foot to the other as she exhales.

'I'm dying for another drink,' she says. 'But I have to take it easy. Terence'll go mad if I get fluthered.'

But she's already very drunk.

After the meal, people begin to filter away. Terence sits at the bar with Hoggy and other men in suits. Una is flushed and talks loudly with her friends. It's almost 7 p.m. by Luke's watch and he slips away.

Back in his father's house Luke idly looks through the books in the cardboard boxes. He recognises some of them: Agatha Christie, Mills & Boon, favourites of his late mother. There's a Bible too and an Irish-English dictionary. Underneath a copy of *Pride and Prejudice* he finds a mottled, black, cloth-covered hardback with faded gold lettering on the spine. *Everything You Always Wanted To Know About Sex* it reads, and, lower down, in tiny writing, the legend *but were afraid to ask*. It opens easily at a dog-eared page. Luke reads the first paragraph and blinks with shock and fresh realisation. The text advises that it's possible for a psychiatrist to turn a homosexual into a happy, well-adjusted heterosexual. Luke trembles as he remembers that awful time — he must have been fifteen — when his father took him to the psychiatrist in Dublin. He remembers his mother crying, his father shouting, 'Give it a rest, woman, for Christ's sake. All I'm trying to do is make him normal.'

There's a knock at the door. It's Jamie.

'Hi there,' he says. He's holding a basket. 'Can I come in?'

'Please do. It's not much of a place.'

'I brought a few bits and pieces.' He puts the basket on the table, takes out two damp bottles of Sauvignon Blanc and two bottles of Rioja. 'Didn't know if you drank white or red,' he grins. Then he takes out napkins, a large packet of potato crisps and some plastic containers filled with food. 'Tortilla, patatas bravas, something with aubergines, squid in chilli sauce, black and green olives,' he recites.

'All this, it must have cost you. Can I give you some money?'

'No problem. I nicked them from your brother's restaurant.'

'That's brilliant. So long as you don't get into trouble.'

'I don't care. You're entitled to some grub from the fuckers anyway. Have you any glasses?'

Luke opens a glass-fronted cabinet. 'Waterford Crystal. Probably never used. Story of their lives,' he says. 'I'll give them a rinse.'

Jamie takes a corkscrew out of his pocket and opens a bottle of white. He pours, they clink glasses and drink.

'This is really good,' says Luke. 'Thank you.'

'It's a pleasure.'

They drink more. Luke finds plates and cutlery and they sit at the table to eat.

'I hate to admit it but Terence's chef isn't bad,' laughs Luke after a while.

'Your brother's an awful prick though.'

'Una is just as bad.'

'She's even worse. She hadn't a clue I was gay when she hired me. I'm guessing she had a fit when she found out.'

'I thought things might have changed.'

'You mean, since they changed the law?' asks Jamie.

'Well, yeah.'

'This place doesn't change much, I can tell you. You wouldn't know whether to laugh or to cry.' Jamie looks glum for a moment. 'No matter,' he says then. 'Let's enjoy ourselves. Have you any music?'

'I don't think... no, wait a minute... ' Luke opens a cupboard and takes out something that looks like a small suitcase. 'Brilliant. It's still here. It's a turntable, believe it or not. It belonged to my mother. I hope it still works.'

He puts it on the floor, plugs it in. Then he finds a pile of LP records in the cupboard, selects *South Pacific* and places it on the turntable.

'I used to love this when I was a kid,' says Luke. 'It's kitsch as hell.'

He carefully places the needle on a vinyl groove. Mitzi Gaynor begins to sing 'I'm Gonna Wash That Man Right Outta My Hair'.

Jamie laughs and pulls Luke up from the couch by one hand. They begin to jive, badly, but soon they are dancing frenetically. They stop only to fill their glasses and to put on more music. They're prancing around the room to tunes from *Showboat* when Luke collapses onto the couch.

'I'm so drunk I can hardly see,' he laughs. 'I have to half-close my eyes.'

Jamie sits down beside him and slowly places a hand on Luke's chest.

They kiss.

After a while the music stops and the needle clicks in the run-off groove until Luke stands up and places it clumsily back on its resting place, scratching the vinyl surface with a ripping sound. Jamie moves toward him again and they go upstairs to lie together on the divan bed.

The thought of sex in his father's house is strange to Luke, and Jamie's body is unfamiliar. It's lean and sinewy, unlike Bernard's warm fleshiness, and his breath smells of cigarettes. Jamie strokes him and kisses him again, licks his ear, presses hard against him.

'What do you prefer,' he whispers. 'Do you like fucking or being fucked?'

'I don't know if I can do anything. I'm just… I'm not right yet.'

'You're kidding. Come on, let's have some fun.'

'I can't.'

'Ah, don't tell me. Everyone I meet these days is still in love with his ex. Christ's sake, get over it. Come on, come on… '

In the morning Jamie is still there, snoring quietly. Luke gets up and dresses. He goes downstairs to the kitchen and fills the kettle. As he places it on the hob, he hears footsteps and turns around. Jamie is standing in the kitchen doorway, fully dressed.

'I'll be off. Sorry if I was a bit pushy last night. Bit too much drink.' He smiles wryly, then turns and walks away. The front door clicks shut.

Luke stands still for a moment, then runs out into the street.

'Jamie,' he shouts. 'Wait.'

Jamie looks back.

'Hang on a second.' Luke rushes back into the house, looks around, picks up the *South Pacific* record and slides it into its cover. Then he grabs a pen and runs out again.

'Here's my contact details,' he says as he writes on the back of the album cover. 'I think you're great, I really do. It's just... My partner died, you see. That's why it's ... difficult.'

Jamie takes the album, kisses Luke on the lips and walks away. He turns around once. 'I'll be in touch,' he says and waves goodbye. Then he's gone.

Luke goes back inside and closes the front door. He walks into the backyard and stands on the cracked concrete, looking out at the garden. As he breathes in, deeply, a ladybird, shiny red with black spots, lands on his sleeve. He doesn't move until it flies away. Finally, he weeps.

ACROSS THE DUCK POND

As the plane began to descend at Shannon airport, I woke to see a patchwork quilt of green fields below. Though I'd married a man from Cork City, I'd never been to Ireland before, and for a moment I wondered if it was real. Towards the back of the plane, a baby began to cry. The lady in the seat next to mine held prayer beads tightly in her hands. Her lips were moving at speed. It seemed we might be in for a rough landing.

Then the plane bumped onto the tarmac once, and once again, before landing safely. Some passengers applauded, probably in relief. Nothing like that happens back home in the States so far as I know, and I wondered if it was an Irish custom.

After trailing through customs and a visit to the restroom, I found a taxi stand outside.

'Heaphy's Car Hire, near Tullyglass,' I said.

'No bother,' said the cab driver. 'I'll have you there in a few minutes.'

Tom Heaphy had the cheapest car rental in Ireland, Liam said, before he died, and you didn't need no credit card either. Seeing as how my credit card was maxed out on account of everything that had happened in the past year, it seemed like a plan. In hindsight, I should have questioned Liam as to how he came by his information, but I wasn't thinking straight at the time.

Outside Heaphys, the air smelled of greenery and smoke, and it was not as cold as I'd feared, but no cars were to be seen in the yard. I thought of walking away, but it was too late — Tom Heaphy had emerged.

Tom was a worn-out man and I could barely understand a word he said. The only car he had was a rust-bucket. It was a stick shift — something I hadn't considered — but three days and a full tank of gas would cost me only fifty euros in cash, so I took it. He gave me a dog-eared road map too, and traced his finger along it to show me the way to Cork. He even drew a rough map in blue on the back of a big white envelope so I'd find Fitzgerald's Park when I got there.

Then I drove without stopping and it rained all the way and the wipers clicked and clacked and everything in that darn car rattled and shook and the engine sounded none too healthy and I was on the wrong side of the road and that stick shift made my left shoulder ache like crazy but I got to Cork in two and half hours — which would have been a miracle if I believed in them.

The heavy rain was still spattering down when I reached Fitzgerald's Park, right near the centre of the city. I turned into a parking space nearby, across the road from an old English-looking house with a red door and a front yard hemmed in by iron railings. By then I was so darn tired I just sat in the car for a while. I didn't feel like ever driving that damn jalopy again.

Do it on a clear day, Liam had said. *On a peaceful day when there's a bit of sun and a slight breeze.*

I remembered how he talked when he lay dying, about the park on a sunny day, filled with green trees and coloured flowers, about the white swans on the river and the ducks on the pond. He talked, too, about the small museum and the teahouse by the gate that served tea and cakes with real whipped cream and strawberry jam. He talked about a time before his mother died and things went bad — but didn't ever say much about why he left Ireland and never went back.

The sky was still grey now, and though the rain had slackened, there was not a hint of sun. I figured that even though it was Ireland in November, it surely could not rain forever and I would soon scatter the ashes and leave. Liam had not been an ideal husband, but he had no other kin as far as I knew. He had made me promise to bring him back to this city, this river. It was his final imposition, knowing that I was a woman of my word.

The grey rain drizzled wearily down and I hoped it would not be long before the sky cleared. *The quicker I can do this thing, the better*, I told myself as I took the urn with Liam's ashes out of my flight bag. Carefully, I wrapped him in my favourite shawl and placed him in the footwell of the front passenger seat. Then I covered him with an old tartan rug I found in the trunk.

When I was done I grabbed my handbag and walked right into the park. I found a restroom in the museum, where I freshened up some. There was a small restaurant in back of it, and though it seemed nothing like the one Liam had described, I went in anyhow, and ordered coffee and a ham sandwich. I got to say I bake a fine rye loaf myself but the bread in that sandwich was just as good as my own, or near enough as makes no difference. I'm a pretty good cook, though I do say so myself. That's how I met Liam, back in Paducah. I was the short order cook in Fast Fred's and he was waiting tables there, working as an illegal. To tell the truth, he was a lousy waiter, but he sure did like to eat. I got to like him, got to like feeding him, and then I got to loving him. Though I knew deep down he was unreliable, I couldn't help myself.

Anyway, the sandwich and the coffee I got in that restaurant went down real good. It was a while since I'd tasted what I ate, so I ordered another. My appetite failed me then. I wrapped the second sandwich in some paper napkins and slipped it in my pocket for later.

Outside, the rain had stopped but the sun sure wasn't shining. The river ran right alongside the park, just like Liam said, and a metal bridge lay beyond. The bridge trembled underfoot as I walked on it, and the grey-brown river flowed below. The Shaky Bridge, Liam had called it and rightly so. I leaned over the rail and I thought, *When the sun comes out, this is the place.* As I stared down into the dark water, it felt strange, as if the river was inviting me to forget why I was there, forget everything, climb over the rail and tumble in. For a moment I wanted to, but I resisted.

Instead, I walked back to the park until I reached the duck pond. That's when I noticed the little girl. I would have liked a little girl, but that's all past me now. She was about eight or nine years old — a cute kid in a pink parka with purple ribbons in her hair — and she was throwing bits of white bread into the water. The ducks propelled themselves towards the pieces, each trying to reach the food before the other, and she was all upset because the bigger ducks were taking the bread she intended for the smaller ones.

'Big bad ducks,' she said. 'Leave some for the little ones.'

I could tell she was frustrated. Frustration, I know about. Try caring for someone who's terminally ill and has no medical insurance in the great You Ess of A. That is frustration.

Two women, younger than me, maybe middle thirties, were standing nearby. One was slim, neat, dark-haired, and she glanced across at the little girl occasionally, so I figured that was her mother. The other was a frowsy blonde. They were talking in such an animated way I knew they had to be talking about men.

'I just think you need a steadier guy, that's all,' the dark-haired one said.

'It's all right for you Claire. You've got Pete and a kid, so you're settled like,' said the blonde. 'But I can't help myself. I'm weak for him. It was all off and then last night he offered me a lift home after work and next thing we were dry-humping in the back seat of his car and now it's kind-of on again...'

The mother, Claire, began to laugh. I wished she'd stop. Love is no laughing matter. It makes you crazy. It makes you do things that don't make sense.

The little girl turned round and shouted, 'Mam! The big ducks are taking all the food from the little ones.'

The mother looked over. 'That's a shame, love,' she said.

I remembered the leftover sandwich in my pocket and had an idea.

'Looky here, I'll distract the big ones,' I told the little girl. I walked round the pond until I was standing right opposite her. Then I took the sandwich from my pocket and threw a piece of it into the congealed water. The bigger ducks sailed across the pond towards me and she watched as they fought among themselves for it. The next time I dropped a piece of bread onto the water, she awaited her chance, and while I kept some of the larger ducks busy, she walked quickly back and forth on her side of the pond, sprinkling crumbs for the ducklings.

'It's working,' she shouted and gave me a thumbs up. 'Good idea!'

Her mother and the other woman smiled at me as they saw the little girl's delight, but soon enough all the bread was gone.

'Right, Gracie,' her mother said then. 'It's time to go home.'

Gracie waved and the women nodded and smiled, as they left the park together. I followed, slowly, behind them. Gracie and her mother stopped at the front gates of the house with the red door—the one right across the street from where I'd parked my rental car. The blonde woman bid them farewell and walked off briskly in the direction of the city centre. Gracie and her mother walked into their yard, climbed up the steps to the red door and went in.

By now it was getting dark and I felt weary so I sat in the car again. I got to thinking about my Aunt Eliza. Eliza was a churchgoing lady, who fed the hungry and tended the sick back in Paducah. She took me in when I got orphaned, and took real good care of me until she died. I figured I was lucky compared to Liam. I missed her.

An old BMW pulled in right next to mine and a large, solid-looking man got out. He locked his car, went across the street, opened the red door with his key and strode in. By the way he did it, like he did that same thing most days, I figured he had to be Claire's husband, and Gracie's father.

Why the heck am I sitting here? I wondered. A part of my head knew the thing to do was drive away and find a cheap hotel for the night, but somehow I could not get going. I turned the heater on and it buzzed and whirred. The car heated up real quick and soon became a dusty warm cocoon. My head began to droop sideways, so I turned the heater off and crawled into the back seat to lie down. Still wearing my coat, I pulled the dusty tartan rug over me and fell asleep to the sound of the rain pattering gently on the car roof.

I dreamt I was sinking into liquorice-black water and woke up scared to death by dark shapes outside the car. Two men were sitting side by side on the hood, smoke swirling from their cigarettes as they laughed and talked. I didn't dare to move and it seemed like forever before they stood up and walked away. My poor old rental car relaxed with a creaking sound and sprung back into its former position.

It was 3 a.m. by my watch now. I must have slept for at least nine hours. The street was damp and shiny and the streetlights made yellow circles at regular intervals along the footpaths.

I sneaked out of the car and into the dark field behind, to pee. Shivering, and hoping no one had seen me, I walked back to the car.

I turned the ignition on and the car heater up full blast. At least I'd saved myself the cost of a room for the night. Surely the sun would come out tomorrow so I could scatter the ashes and leave. If only Liam had died in August, not November. The only thing that comforted me was the lighted window upstairs in the house with the red door across the street.

In the morning, I slunk out into the rain. In the museum, I used the restroom and cleaned up a little. Afterwards, I ordered juice and coffee and a panini in the café, before going back to the car to wait.

Once, that morning, I thought I saw a glimmer of sun behind a cloud, but I was wrong. I wrapped myself in the old tartan rug and lost myself in terrible memories. I half-knew I was acting like a crazy person and that I might end up living in the goddam car at this rate, but I felt powerless to make any drastic move. It was as if I lived in some kind of foggy dream in which it was beyond me to make any decision other than to wait and wait while the rain drummed hard on the car roof. *Nothing lasts forever*, I told myself. I waited.

In the afternoon, the rain eased a little. I pushed my unwilling body out of the car and forced myself to walk towards the city. I needed to eat — just a little something to keep me going. I stopped at a fast food restaurant and ordered a burger, but as I ate, the girl at the table next to mine reminded me of a skinny wall-eyed waitress that Liam once cheated on me with. I got to feeling mad and bitter and tired of it all. *The hell with it*, I thought. *I'll throw his ashes over the bridge any old way. It's more than he deserves.*

The Shaky Bridge quivered as I walked along. I stopped midway and balanced that darn urn on the railing, but the sky was so deadly grey that I didn't have the heart to scatter him like that after all. Instead, I replaced the cover on the urn and walked back across the trembling bridge.

In the park, the children's playground stood deserted; the bright reds and yellows and blues of its slides and swings and roundabouts glistened wet and childless in the drizzling rain. I paused nearby, on the path that ran along the river's edge, and once again I considered throwing Liam into the water right there.

As I hesitated by the river bank, a swan floated by, neck lowered, all graceful and dignified, and she — for I was convinced it was a she — raised her head to stare at me gravely.

'Hey you, Missus Swan,' I said, bitterly. 'Did you lose your husband too? I hope he wasn't a goddam fool like mine.'

Then it came to me that, apart from the briefest words to airport staff and shop assistants and old Tom Heaphy the car hire man and Gracie the little girl in the park — and now, Missus Swan — I had not spoken to a living soul in days.

'You shithead,' I told Liam as I put him back in the car, remembering his jaunty, careless, faithless ways and all the pain he'd caused me. Then I recalled the fear in those grey eyes when he came back to me for help, so I wrapped the shawl around him all the same.

In a nearby liquor store, I bought a bottle of red wine and some savoury snacks and had me a little party in my car and listened to the radio before I rolled into the back seat and fell asleep again.

It was 3 a.m. when I awoke. A man in a tuxedo was knocking on the red door.

'Wake up, Pete,' he hollered.

The little girl's father appeared, in pyjamas, on the doorstep.

I sat up and pushed between the seats until I was back in the driver's seat, then rolled the window slowly down so I could hear.

'Thing is, Pete, the road seems to be flooding,' the tuxedo man slurred. 'You might want to move your car.'

He walked unsteadily back to his own car and got in, before driving very slowly towards the city, water rippling in his wake.

Pete walked out into the street. It was no longer a street but a shallow stream.

'Oh Christ,' he said and ran back into the house.

When he came out again he was wearing rubber boots. He went straight to his car, which was still parked right next to mine. I sat very still so he wouldn't notice me. As he turned on the ignition, the woman called Claire emerged.

'Oh my God,' she said, and went back inside.

Next time she emerged, she was wearing rubber boots too. She paddled along the pavement and unlocked a double gate next to the house. Pete drove slowly into the street and reversed through the gate until I could no longer see his car.

Claire sloshed through the rising water to ring the doorbell of the house beyond and then the next. The neighbours came out and stood for a while under the streetlights, talking in worried tones as they watched the water rise.

'It's getting higher,' I heard Pete say.

'I wonder if we should start moving furniture,' said someone else.

The little girl appeared in the open doorway. She wore patterned red pyjamas and held a small brown bear.

'What about the lady?' the little girl said. 'She'll get really wet.'

'What lady?' said Pete.

'The lady over there in her car. She needs to come inside.'

They all looked across at me. I sat there in the driver's seat, not knowing where to look.

'Jesus love, we don't know the woman from Adam,' I heard Pete say.

The little girl was stubborn. 'She's a nice lady. She helped us to feed the baby ducks.'

'That's right,' said Claire. 'She can't stay out here.'

Then came a rushing sound like the sea.

'God Almighty, the dam must have burst—there's a wave coming up the street,' Pete said.

I fumbled for the key and turned on the ignition. A blinking light appeared on the dashboard. Claire waded across the street and leaned down to talk to me through the open car window. 'Hello there. I'm

Claire. I live across the road. You need to come in for a while. There's a flood, you see. The water is rising.'

'Thank you kindly, Ma'am,' I said. 'But I'm just about leaving now.'

The little girl was hopping up and down on the doorstep. Claire looked back at her. 'Stay inside, Gracie,' she commanded. She turned back to me. 'You'll be safer inside,' she said.

I shook my head, turned on the headlights and drove slowly into the road. The car was making a loud bleeping sound and several lights were flashing on the dashboard now. In my rear mirror I could see Claire struggling back to her house through the rising water. Anyway, I revved up and kept going until the damn car slowed down and stopped right there in the middle of what used to be the street. I tried to restart it again and again but the engine refused to turn.

There was nothing to do but step out of the car. Shocking ice-cold water was up to my knees. Flowing toward the city, the road was a river now. I leaned back in to grab my handbag from the front seat. I hung it round my neck by its strap. *The car might float away,* I thought. *I can't leave anything behind.* I waded to the trunk. My flight bag was in there. I tugged at the zip and shoved my handbag inside. I zipped the holdall back up and slung it over my shoulder. I slammed the trunk shut.

Then I remembered Liam and groaned. I struggled back around to the passenger side to rescue the urn. It was goddamn hard to force open the door but I managed, at last.

The urn was in the foot well of the passenger seat, still wrapped in my shawl. As I grasped it with both hands and lifted it up, the rushing water unbalanced me for a moment. The urn slipped through the shawl and out of my hands. As it slid into the water, the lid fell off. The shawl dangled limp and useless in my hands. Liam's ashes drifted away on the floodwaters. There was no sun, no light breeze, only water and more water and rain and more rain and I stood there, furious, in the freezing, swirling water and I swore like a sailor, with every vicious word I could think of. Livid with rage, I cussed Liam for not keeping up the payments on his medical plan like he was supposed to. I screamed at him for being unreliable and weak, for leaving me nothing but debts and pain. I cried for him and raved at him for having the damn gall to float right away after all my trouble and because I had nothing left now, not even ashes, and because of all the wasted years—and because I was crazy enough to love him still.

Then I knew I had to move.

As I struggled to walk back to the house with the red door, my face was wet from tears and the ice-cold water was rising fast but a light in the window pulled me forward against the current.

By the time I reached their house it was raining again and water was lapping against the top step. When I rang the doorbell, the red door swung open and warm air flowed out—and in spite of all that had occurred, their hallway floor was dry.

The little girl, Gracie, danced about the hall, saying, 'Gosh you're so wet!' My sodden shoes and trousers dripped puddles on the tiled floor and I longed to wipe them dry. The mother, Claire, seemed to understand my discomfort.

'No trouble,' she said. 'Would you like to dry off and maybe have a shower?'

Before I knew it I was alone in a warm bathroom, holding a large towel, my flight bag right beside me on the floor.

Afterwards, it felt mighty strange to be dressed in clean dry clothes. My lank wet hair seemed longer than before, and my face in the mirror was at once both older and younger than the last time I had bothered to look.

When I emerged, quietly, from the bathroom, Gracie was sitting on the stairs outside.

'Mam says I must show you where you're going to sleep,' she said.

I followed her, my flight bag in one hand and my sodden

belongings in the other. She hopped busily up the stairs in her soft red pyjamas, patterned with tiny brown bears.

At the top of the house was a small box room with a slanting roof. The room contained a single bed and a wooden chair. In the corner, damp clothes hung on a wooden rack next to a blue laundry basket heaped with a motley collection of un-ironed clothes.

Claire appeared in the doorway.

'Thought you might need this,' she said. She handed me a hair dryer. 'Gracie, I've left some warm milk in your room. Drink it, then go right back to sleep.'

'I won't be able to go to school tomorrow, will I?' Gracie asked.

'You won't,' said Claire. 'And it's tomorrow already. Still, you need to sleep for a few hours now or you'll just get over-tired.' She turned to me then and said, 'Come downstairs when you're ready. I'll put the kettle on.'

I stood in the doorway of the big kitchen. Claire was sitting at a wooden table, writing a list on a sheet of paper. Pete was standing nearby talking into a mobile phone. He looked angry and I felt afraid, for the first time.

'What do you mean, you know nothing? You're the police, for God's sake,' he shouted into the phone.

Claire noticed me then. 'Come in,' she smiled and waved me towards the chair next to her.

'Well, get onto it, then!' said Pete. He put the phone down and looked at Claire. 'Unbelievable. Guess what the langer in the cop station said. "Flood, what flood?" This country. You gotta laugh.' Then he looked at me. 'You know something?' he said. 'A hot toddy would do us all the world of good.'

I had not heard of this drink before, so I watched carefully as Pete put a teaspoon into each of three glasses. In each glass he dissolved brown sugar in boiling water and added a crescent of yellow lemon studded with cloves and a generous measure of Irish whiskey. I'm not a bourbon drinker but it seemed rude to refuse. Besides, the fragrance of those cloves and lemon slices made it seem more like good medicine than liquor. Anyhow, I was glad that I'd accepted. That first hot toddy warmed my bones and steadied me.

'This is the finest beverage I ever had,' I told him. He and Claire laughed and insisted I should have another.

Now and then Pete went out to the hallway and opened the front door. Each time he returned he looked a little less anxious.

'Doesn't seem to be rising any more,' he said. 'Maybe we'll be alright.'

Claire made grilled cheese sandwiches with onion and tomato. She cut them in triangles and called them 'toasted cheesies'. They tasted mighty fine and I told her so.

The fact that I had hardly spoken to a soul since Liam's funeral, along with the alcohol, turned me dizzy and talkative. By the time Pete placed a third hot whiskey drink before me, I felt right at home.

'I guess I should explain what I been doing around here,' I said.

'That's your own business,' said Pete, careful-like, looking at me across the table.

'Go on,' said Claire. 'You can tell us.'

So I told them about Liam dying and wanting me to bring his ashes home to Ireland.

'I'm sorry for your trouble,' said Pete.

'You poor thing,' said Claire. She looked like she was going to cry and her face looked sort of comical in its sorrow.

In fact, they both looked so sad I felt like I should tell them more. I remembered the photo and took it out of my bag to show them. It was an old photo of Liam and I, from back when we first met, long before the divorce. He looked uneasily respectable in his only suit, and older than me (he was, by nine years). I looked so young, for all the world as if I was the one who needed rescuing, when all along it had been him.

'He came to Kentucky for the horses,' I explained. 'He loved horses. He worked on one of the big stud farms in Lexington until he had an accident. After that, he couldn't ride any more and ended up waiting on tables in a diner in Paducah. I was a chef there, so that's how we met.'

They both seemed interested, so I carried on.

'He had only bad memories of Ireland, apart from Fitzgerald's Park. He always remembered being there when he was real young, on a fine sunny day with his mother. Then his mother died and he ended up in Juvie.'

'Juvie?' Claire asked.

'Juvenile Hall,' I explained. 'I don't know what you all call it here.'

'An industrial school?' Pete suggested.

'Maybe. He didn't say much, but I got the impression it was real bad, a prison for kids. Soon as he got out of there, he left Ireland and he never went back.'

'Industrial schools were awful places. Orphans and illegitimate kids got shunted into them,' Claire said. She began to talk of Goldenbridge. 'Such a pretty name, but what an evil place. In Goldenbridge, the children had an awful life. They spent their days making rosary beads and they were only half-fed. A cousin of mine ended up there,' Claire added. 'I only met her recently. I feel awful for her. She's very damaged, but no wonder.'

'Liam was a troubled person also,' I said. 'Fact is, he was a trial to me.'

I didn't say how much of a trial. I didn't like to disrespect him, even now, in front of people who had never known him. I carried on and told them about the journey and how I'd waited for the sun to shine.

'You'd have some wait for sun in November around here,' Pete commented.

'So where *did* you scatter the ashes in the end?' asked Claire.

I began to explain and when it came to the point where the urn slipped out of my hands, I was about ready to cry but I tried to keep a grip on myself. Then, I heard a choking sound from Claire and I looked at her and her face was so sad it was almost comical again and her hand was across her mouth and she began to heave with laughter as tears flowed down her face — and then I was laughing too, laughing hysterically through my tears.

Pete looked aghast. 'Stop it, Claire,' he said.

'I'm so sorry,' Claire said, gasping for breath. 'I'm mortified. It just came over me and I couldn't stop. It gets me that way sometimes. You should have seen me at my father's funeral.'

'She won't have a clue what you're on about,' said Pete.

'But I do,' I said. And I did.

By now, there was hardly any whiskey left. Pete said we should use the last of it to drink a toast to Liam. Glasses in hands, we went to the front door. We huddled together on the top step and stared out at the flood. Claire was sure the water had gone down. Pete merely said it hadn't risen any higher. The rain had stopped, at last, and a grey dawn was breaking.

'Well, your Liam is out here somewhere,' said Pete.

'May he rest in peace,' said Claire.

They clinked their glasses against mine and I nodded, unable to speak. I drained my glass, swallowing hard.

Pete sighed. 'You come all this way, you do all you can, and at the last lap it all goes haywire,' he said, shaking his head. 'But sure, isn't that life for you, ha?'

'Things never worked out where Liam was involved,' I said.

'You must remember, you did the best you could,' said Claire, and she hugged me. 'Now I'm off to bed.'

'I'm going to hit the hay too,' Pete declared. 'If you're up before us, help yourself to food. There's porridge and eggs and stuff.'

'No bread though,' warned Claire. 'We finished the sliced pan. I might try to bake soda bread tomorrow.'

'I could do that,' I offered. 'If you'd let me.'

'You're a chef,' Pete remembered. 'Sure, baking a loaf is no bother to this lady, Claire.'

'Great. I'm hopeless at baking. There's flour and things in the cupboard.' Claire waved a hand vaguely back towards the kitchen. 'Night,' she said. 'See you in the morning. Or maybe the afternoon.'

Pete said goodnight too and followed her up the stairs.

I was not sleepy. Time meant nothing to me. I felt as if I would never need to sleep again.

Bread. I could make bread. I went back into the kitchen. Quietly, so as not to wake anyone, I searched for ingredients. There was flour but no yeast. I found baking soda at the back of a cupboard and reckoned I could remember how to make Irish soda bread. Years back, I used to make it sometimes, for Liam. I switched the oven on and greased the surface of a baking tray with some butter. I soured a jug of milk with a tablespoon of lemon juice. I sifted flour and salt and a teaspoon of baking soda into a white earthenware bowl. Little by little, I poured in the soured milk and mixed it into dough. I sprinkled a cloud of flour onto the wooden work surface, turned the dough out and kneaded it gently. I placed the dough on the baking tray and cut a gentle cross in the centre. Then I put it in the oven and set the timer. It was 5.35 a.m. by my watch, but it could have been any time at all.

I cleared the table then. I washed the glasses and the plates, the cutlery, everything. I dried them all and put away what I could. I wiped down all the kitchen surfaces. It was still only 5.55 a.m. I checked the bread in the oven and decided it needed a few minutes more.

I wandered out to the front door and opened it again. Outside, the road was still a river, but now there was scarcely a ripple in the water. The early morning sky was calm and blue. Up the street a ways, two parked cars stood door-handle deep in water, and something yellow — perhaps a child's plastic toy — bobbed quietly by.

As I stood there, looking out at the floodwaters, a white swan came into view. She floated in the water right outside the front railings of the house. For some reason, I was convinced that this was the self-same swan I'd spoken to, the day before. Missus Swan, if it were she, looked tranquil as she gazed at me. The thought struck me that, for the first time ever, Missus Swan was able to float along this street and look right in, real close, at how we humans live. I fancied she was savouring the moment.

'Fare well,' I said to Missus Swan and saluted her for her gumption.

I went inside and shut the door. Back in the kitchen, the oven timer pinged. It was time to rescue the bread.

ACKNOWLEDGEMENTS

Acknowledgements are due to the following publications in which versions of these stories have appeared, or will appear: *Sunday Tribune*; *Sharp Sticks, Driven Nails* (Stinging Fly Press); *Etherbooks*; *Irish Examiner*; *Necessary Fiction*; *Irish Independent*; *The Penny Dreadful*; *Long Story, Short Literary Journal*; *Lakeview International Journal of Literature and Arts*; and *Braids: A Global Anthology of Short Stories*.

I would like to express my sincere thanks to the following organisations for their support and encouragement: Hennessy Literary Awards; the Arts Council of Ireland; Cork City Council; The School of English, University College, Cork; Munster Literature Centre; Triskel Arts Centre; Cork City Library; Bantry Library; the Heinrich Böll Association; Ó Bhéal; and, of course, my publishers, Lisa Frank and John Walsh of Doire Press.

I am grateful to Nick Kelly for allowing me to use a line from one of his songs in 'Is This Like Scotland?'.

Many thanks to John and Billie MacMonagle of Raven Design.

I would also like to thank Claire Keegan for her kind encouragement.

I wish to thank Colette Sheridan, William Wall, Liz Kirwan, Claire Connolly, Paul O'Donovan, Conal Creedon, Fiona O'Toole, Catherine Kirwan, Philip Ó Ceallaigh, Audrey Brennan, Tara Quirke, Isobel Creed, Brenda Wilson Wooley, Kieran O'Connor and many others— too numerous to mention individually—for their kindness and support.

My thanks are also due to my dear parents, Sally and Michael D'Arcy, to my brother Mike D'Arcy and to my sister Mary D'Arcy.

Last, but not least, thanks and love to my husband Andrew Lane and my son Cass D'Arcy Lane.

MADELEINE D'ARCY was born in Ireland. She spent thirteen years in the UK, where she worked as a criminal legal aid solicitor and as a legal editor in London. Returning to Cork city in 1999 with her husband and son, she worked as a solicitor in the Refugee Legal Service. In 2010 she received a Hennessy X.O Literary Award for First Fiction as well as the overall Hennessy X.O Literary Award for New Irish Writer. Her stories have been short-listed and commended in many competitions, including the William Trevor/Elizabeth Bowen Short Story Competition, Fish Short Story Prize, the Bridport Prize and the Seán Ó Faoláin Short Story Competition.

Madeleine has been awarded bursaries by the Arts Council of Ireland and by Cork City Council. She is a member of Cork Screenwriting Group, and a short film of her story 'Dog Pound', featuring the distinguished Irish actor Frank Kelly, was made in 2014. Madeleine is currently a scholarship student on the inaugural MA in Creative Writing 2013-2014 in University College Cork. *Waiting for the Bullet* is her first collection of short fiction.

Other Fiction Titles by Doire Press

End of Days by Aileen Armstrong
Fireproof and other Stories by Celeste Augé
Lights in the Distance by Susan Millar DuMars
Killer à la Carte by Gerry Galvin
And by Jim Mullarkey
Border Lines by John Walsh

Galway Stories edited by Lisa Frank
30 under 30 edited by Elizabeth Reapy